"Let go of your fear, Victoria."

Dirk's voice was husky. The searing fire of his kiss started off a sweet consuming ache in Victoria's limbs. The temptation of his caressing touch was potent.

"No," she choked out. "I'm sure it would make quite an exclusive story to have bedded Charles Beaumont's daughter, but that's one story you're not going to get."

"It would probably make a hell of a story," he snapped, glaring at her in surprise, "but I don't write for the scandal sheets. In fact, I'd forgotten you were even related to Charles Beaumont!"

Victoria wished she could believe him, but he had her so mixed up she didn't know what she wanted anymore—unless it was the peace she had known before Dirk entered her life!

JANET DAILEY AMERICANA

Every novel in this collection is your passport to a romantic tour of the United States through time-honored favorites by America's First Lady of romance fiction. Each of the fifty novels is set in a different state, researched by Janet and her husband, Bill. For the Daileys it was an odyssey of discovery. For you, it's the journey of a lifetime.

The state flower depicted on the cover of this book is apple blossom.

Janet Dailey Americana

Don't miss any of our special offers. Write to us at the following address for information on our newest releases.

Harlequin Reader Service
901 Fuhrmann Blvd., P.O. Box 1397, Buffalo, NY 14240
Canadian address: P.O. Box 603,
Fort Erie, Ont. L2A 5X3

ENEMY IN CAMP

Harlequin Books

TORONTO • NEW YORK • LONDON
AMSTERDAM • PARIS • SYDNEY • HAMBURG
STOCKHOLM • ATHENS • TOKYO • MILAN

Janet Dailey Americana edition published April 1987
ISBN 373-89822-3

Harlequin Presents edition published August 1980

Original hardcover edition published in 1980
by Mills & Boon Limited

CHAPTER ONE

THE TAXI went as fast as the traffic on the boulevard of Jefferson Avenue would allow. Ahead rose the gleaming structure of the Renaissance Center, part of the rebirth of downtown Detroit. The seventy-story cylindrical tower of the Plaza Hotel dominated its four sister towers that surrounded it like ladies-in-waiting. The monolith of modern architecture overlooked the Detroit River, the Canadian province of Ontario on its opposite shore, and the expanse of water to the northeast called Lake St. Clair.

Under a red light, the taxi driver slowed the cab to a stop at the intersection of the entrance driveway to the Renaissance Center and glanced in the rearview mirror at his female passenger. "We're almost there, miss," he announced and noticed her glance at the delicate gold watch on her wrist. "I told you we'd make it in no time flat."

"Yes, you did." The smile Victoria Beaumont gave him was vaguely absent, but not a glimmer of her inner impatience was visible in her expression.

The cabbie didn't mind the faint disinterest of her smile. He liked the sound of her voice, so calm and well educated. Not that she had talked to him much. Other than confiding that she was late for a luncheon appointment at the Renaissance Center and would he please hurry, she hadn't volunteered any conversation except to make polite responses to him. He'd done all the talking.

"I wouldn't worry about him bein' upset. As soon as he sees you he'll forget that you're late." There was no doubt in the cab driver's mind that his attractive passenger was meeting a man for lunch.

He silently wished he was ten years younger, forty pounds lighter and possessed a head full of hair. The stack of packages and dress boxes on the seat beside her indicated he would also need a fat wallet, but the cabbie overlooked that.

"I'm not so certain about that," Victoria replied, choosing not to disabuse his impression she was meeting a man.

"If he don't, then he don't know a good thing when he sees it," the cab driver insisted and unabashedly studied her profile in his mirror.

Her complexion looked smooth and soft to him, with a faint golden tinge from the sun even though it was only May. She had nice cheekbones, and a perfect nose, too, not too straight and not too short. Her mouth was sensational, soft and shiny from some dusty-rose lipstick. He'd been around enough to know she was something special.

"Are you a model?" he asked.

"No." Victoria didn't volunteer the information that she was a member of the idle rich—which was a fallacy—the rich were never idle. Their appointment calendars were always filled with charity meetings, social clubs, tennis dates, and a variety of parties, all of which could become terribly boring.

"You sure got the looks for it," the cabbie replied. "I oughta know. I get all kinds of passengers in my cab from hookers—beggin' your pardon—to housewives. But you're different. You got class, you know? I mean, you ain't the kind of woman a guy makes fresh remarks to."

"Thank you." Victoria was certain there was a compliment in there somewhere, but it was a struggle to keep back the bubble of amused laughter. Her eyes were dancing with it, though, and she looked out the window so he wouldn't think she was laughing at him.

"It ain't just the way you smell," he assured her, having been enveloped in the sensual cloud of her expensive perfume since she had entered his cab. "It's the color of your hair. On any other woman it'd probably be called a washed-out brown, but on you it looks blond. What color do you call it?"

"I don't know." Victoria had never had to label it before. It was much too light to be considered brown and lacked the golden cast to be a true blond. "Biscuit-colored, I suppose."

"Yeah, I guess," the driver agreed after a moment's hesitation. "And there's the way you got it fixed, too. When my wife goes to a beauty shop, she either comes out lookin' like a poodle or else like she's had her hair starched. Even though your hair ain't long it looks loose and casual, sorta windswept. It doesn't make a guy think he'll ruin it if he touches it, you know?"

"Yes, I think I do," Victoria murmured to disguise her amusement. The cabbie was so engrossed in her reflection she had to call his attention to the traffic light. "It's changing to green."

"Right," he answered in a voice that pretended he had known it all along.

When the traffic ahead of him moved out of the way, he turned the cab into the drive and stopped at one of the entrances of the center. Moving agilely for a man his size and age, he was out of the cab and around to the rear passenger door to help Victoria out, assisting her with a gallantry that was more touching than amusing.

"Thank you." Victoria added a generous tip to the fare.

"You're welcome." He began hauling out her packages and garment boxes from the rear seat. "You want some help with this?"

"I think I can manage." It took some maneuvering to slip her fingers through all the plastic grips, but she succeeded with help from the cab driver. "What time is it?"

"Half past one. And you tell that guy if he's upset with you for bein' late, there's plenty of other fellas that'd be happy to be in his shoes."

"I'll remember that." This time there was nothing distracted about the smile lighting her face.

The driver started toward the entrance door to open it for her and stopped. "What color are your eyes?" His own narrowed on her with puzzled intensity.

"Gray."

An audible breath of amazement came from his throat. "I never knew anybody with gray eyes before." It was said to himself as he moved to hold the door for her. "If you ever need a cab again, miss, you just call up and ask for Joe Kopacek. That's Czech," he identified the nationality of his name.

"I'll remember, Mr. Kopacek," Victoria promised with a faint nod that unknowingly resembled an imperial acknowledgement.

Inside the entrance, Victoria was confronted by a labyrinth of corridors connecting a multistoried center of shops. It didn't seem to matter how many times she came to the center she still had difficulty orienting herself. Standing by a wall was a uniformed man, a security guard.

"Excuse me, could you direct me to the restaurant?" she requested with a formal smile touching her lips.

"Which restaurant?" he grinned at her question. "I think there are fourteen in this complex."

"Lord!" It was a muffled exclamation of irritation. Victoria couldn't remember a specific one being stated now, so she opted for the one where they usually lunched when they were downtown. "The hotel has a terrace-type café, doesn't it? Near the elevators?"

"Yes," the guard nodded and pointed to the corridor on Victoria's right. "Go that way and keep to your left. You can't miss it."

"Thank you."

Victoria followed his directions and arrived at the open center of the complex. It was an ultramodern area of layered, curving, rising buttresses of concrete, its bland sterility alleviated by the abundant usage of potted plants and trees. Crisscrossing walkways and escalators connected one side to the other and one level to the next. At a bottom level was the restaurant Victoria was seeking. The impression was one of a sidewalk café, except that it was in the center of the complex and merely cordoned off from the rest of the lobby.

Making her way to the restaurant entrance of bamboo screens Victoria scanned the tables. The hostess approached to inquire, "How many, please?"

"I'm meeting someone here," Victoria explained and caught sight of a familiar brown-haired woman seated alone at one of the tables with her back to the entrance. "There she is."

With a brief smile of dismissal to the hostess she wove her way through the tables. The boxes and packages in her hands made her progress slow to avoid bumping into those seated at the tables. When she reached the one where the woman was sitting, Victoria stopped to begin piling her packages in an empty chair.

"Hello, mom. Had you given up on me?" Victoria greeted her with a direct reference to her tardiness. "I lost all track of time, I'm afraid."

"As long as it was only time that you lost, and not one or two packages along the way," Lena Beaumont announced with a dryly indulgent look at all the parcels.

Victoria simply laughed at that and sat in the chair next to her mother. "I see that I missed dad." She observed the used coffee cup and crumpled napkin at the place setting opposite her.

"Yes, he had an appointment and couldn't wait."

The waitress appeared to give Victoria a menu and offer her coffee. "No, thank you. Iced tea, please," she requested and began to peruse the fare. "What did you and dad have, mom?"

"I had a club sandwich and your father had soup and some kind of fish." There was a subdued gleam in the gray eyes that were very much the same color as her daughter's, although age had given them the glint of wisdom.

"Mmm." It was a noncommittal sound Victoria made. When the waitress returned she closed the menu and ordered, "Spinach salad with very little dressing—low calorie if you have it."

"Yes, ma'am," the waitress nodded and collected the menu before moving away.

"You have more willpower than I do, Tory," her mother sighed. "You should loan me some of yours so I can get rid of this extra fifteen pounds I'm carrying around."

"On you it looks good," Victoria insisted. Both were the same height and the same approximate build. Despite the extra weight, her mother still possessed the necessary feminine curves, but no one would ever accuse her of being heavy.

"Spoken like a diplomatic daughter," Lena Beaumont laughed.

"On the subject of looking good, wait until you see the clothes I found." With a flick of her long fingers, Victoria gestured toward the packages piled in the chair near her.

"What did you do, purchase a new summer wardrobe? I know you 'don't have a thing to wear,' " her mother teased on a dry note.

"It isn't so far from the truth," Victoria defended. "There are a lot of clothes in my closet, but most of them are very juvenile in style. I am twenty-three. It's time I began dressing like it."

"Yes, that's very old," she mocked.

"No, it isn't," Victoria refused to rise to the bait. "And you know very well what I mean. Most of my clothes have been more fad fashion than style fashion. Adrianne was mentioning the other day that the second-hand clothes shop needed donations desperately, so I thought I'd clean out my closet and take what I don't want anymore to the shop."

"That's an excellent idea," her mother agreed.

"I thought so." Victoria paused, her gray eyes resting on the drink glass with its olive on the bottom that sat where her father had been.

"What's this? A martini lunch? That isn't like dad."

"He was celebrating."

"What?" Victoria lifted a finely arched brow, not finding any particular significance in her memory for this particular day in May.

"He persuaded Dirk Ramsey to spend a couple of weeks with us at Mackinac Island this June," Lena Beaumont explained.

"He what?" Her astonishment bordered on incredulity. "Why on earth is that something to celebrate? And why would he want to persuade that sniping, vicious . . . ." Victoria couldn't find adjectives vile enough to describe the political journalist whose syndicated column appeared in all the major newspapers in the country, and several abroad.

"Keep your voice down, Tory," her mother reproved.

"I don't particularly care who knows what I think of that poor excuse for a reporter who makes his living out of impugning other people's character." Victoria lowered her volume, but not the venom of her tone. "Look at the innuendos he has made against dad in his column. They were virtually lies!"

"There was just enough truth in them to make them undeniable," Lena reminded her.

"That is precisely my point. This Dirk Ramsey interprets things in the way that is the most damaging. What does he know about dad? Oh, they may have seen each other once or twice, but dad admitted that they had never even been introduced!'' Victoria flared. ''Yet Ramsey has practically accused dad of being the puppeteer who pulls the strings in the governor's mansion. He has hinted that dad's sense of civic responsibility is motivated by greed. And he has insinuated that dad's interest in national affairs is an attempt to have a private back door to the White House, or else a justiceship on the Supreme Court! It's sickening what that man gets away with in print.''

''Tory, you are old enough to be aware that your father is not only wealthy, he is also very influential,'' her mother began in a reasoning tone.

But Victoria wasn't to be reasoned with. Her eyes were the turbulent gray of storm clouds rolling in from the lakes. ''His legal firm is also one of the most respected in the state, possibly in the country. When dad was actively practicing law he was one of the best attorneys. I fully understand that since he has become politically involved it's natural for him to come under public scrutiny. I don't object to that. I object to some stranger maligning his integrity.''

''That is precisely your father's point.'' Lena Beaumont paused and held up a silencing forefinger as the waitress arrived with Victoria's salad and freshened her mother's cup of coffee. Victoria kept quiet while the waitress was there, but it was a simmering quiet.

''What is 'precisely' his point?'' she demanded when the girl had gone, attacking the salad with a vengeance.

"That Dirk Ramsey doesn't know him," her mother explained. "Your father has always made it a point to be open with the press. On several occasions he has gone out of his way to cultivate their respect. The last thing he wants or needs is to become involved in a feud with a national journalist like Dirk Ramsey."

"Journalist—he doesn't deserve the term. He has climbed to the top by tarnishing images of public figures," Victoria snapped. "I wouldn't call him famous. Notorious is more appropriate."

"It doesn't matter whether you consider him famous or notorious. Whatever Dirk Ramsey prints or says, people pay attention to it." Lena Beaumont continued on her reasoning tactic.

"In my opinion dad should sue him." Victoria stabbed at a dark green spinach leaf with her fork.

"That would be jumping from the frying pan into the fire. It isn't possible to attack one member of the press without the others leaping to his defense. Instead of having one man against him, your father would have them all," was the dry retort.

"So if you can't beat them, join them. Is that his plan of attack?" Victoria knew she sounded sarcastic and didn't care.

Until Dirk Ramsey had begun making questionable references to her father in his column, Victoria had never even read it. After reading two columns of his interpretations of half-truths, she refused to even look at it again. Once she had heard him introduced on some national television show and immediately switched channels. One glimpse of his arrogantly handsome face was all she had needed to convince her he was only seeking his own glory.

"Essentially, it is," her mother agreed with her comment. "Dirk Ramsey doesn't know your father. He's barely exchanged ten words with him. So your father contacted him and suggested they become better acquainted. He invited him to spend two weeks with us at Mackinac Island for that purpose and Mr. Ramsey accepted."

"It's absurd. It's absolutely absurd!" Victoria set her fork down to confront her mother.

"It's perfectly reasonable. Once Dirk Ramsey gets to know your father, he will see for himself that Charles is simply not the way he's been depicted."

"And if he doesn't see it, what then?" Victoria challenged.

"Then it won't be because your father failed to try to change his mind." She sipped at her coffee with a calmness that Victoria had so often envied and tried to emulate.

"Dad can't be serious." Victoria shook her head, waves of her medium-length beige hair brushing her neck. "He could accomplish the same thing by having dinner with the man or playing a couple of rounds of golf or tennis."

"No, he couldn't," Lena Beaumont denied that suggestion. "Dirk Ramsey would suspect that your father was putting up a facade. But nobody can maintain a facade for two weeks, day in and day out."

"Wait a minute." Victoria straightened, eyeing her mother with suspicion. "When you said dad invited Ramsey to Mackinac Island, you didn't mean that he would be staying with us—at our summer home? He will be staying at a hotel, won't he?"

"Of course not," her mother laughed. "He will be our guest, just like anyone else we would invite."

"That's even worse!" she declared. "It's like inviting your enemy into camp to inspect your defenses!"

"You are exaggerating, Tory," her mother sighed with some amusement.

"I'm not. If you don't see it, dad should," she insisted. "Can you imagine how a man like Ramsey can twist even the most insignificant thing?"

"It's up to all of us to persuade him that he has formed a misconception," Lena reasoned.

"You can't be serious, mother," Victoria replied with some disgust. "You know the stage Penny is in," she said, referring to her sixteen-year-old sister. "She knows everything. She's always talking back, sassing. Can you imagine the kind of impression she is going to give Ramsey?"

"Penny wants to be treated like an adult. So, we will sit down and discuss this with her. Explain that we will expect her to behave with the family interest as her prime consideration."

Lena Beaumont refused to be as pessimistic as her daughter.

"With our luck, Penny will meet some radical student and start picketing the house," Victoria muttered.

"The way you did," her mother suggested with a definite sparkle in her eyes.

"Please, don't remind me of that embarrassing episode in my life." The heightened color in her cheeks had nothing to do with the tint of blusher.

"Let's see. If I recall correctly, you were accusing your father of—I don't remember exactly how your sign was worded—but it was something to do with making too much money and thus depriving the poor. At the same time, you were trying to persuade him to raise your allowance." Lena paused, a smiling frown dominating her expression. "What was the name of that boy who instigated that rebellion?"

"I don't remember his name. Everyone called him by his nickname, Lightning." In spite of herself Victoria felt a smile teasing at the corners of her mouth. It quickly became cynical as another thought flashed across her mind. "I can guess how Ramsey would twist that silly incident." She heard the impatient sound her mother made. "If Dirk Ramsey accepted dad's invitation, you can bet he wasn't motivated by a desire to get to the truth. He'll be gathering more ammunition for another attack. I'm sure he jumped at the opportunity to unearth any skeleton in the closet, and if he can't find one he'll invent it," Victoria declared, snapping a rye cracker in half.

"You are prejudging him, Tory," her mother pointed out. "The very thing that you are accusing him of doing."

"Oh, yes, he has prejudged us," she nodded with simmering anger. "I believe he suggested once that we were a family of snobs, too good to mingle with the rest of the world. Dad has disproved that, hasn't he? Who could personify that ilk more than Dirk Ramsey?"

"Your attitude is wrong, Tory," her mother reproved. "You need to keep an open mind about this."

"I prefer to keep my eyes open," she retorted. "Snobs, indeed! I have never considered myself to be better than anyone else. I have had more advantages than others because of the accident of my birth to you and dad, but I am fully aware that I could have been our waitress. I don't think less of her because of her employment. It could easily be me. We don't belong to exclusive clubs because they keep out the riffraff. We go to them because they are close to our home, or because our friends belong to them, or some equally innocent reason."

"I know that, dear." Lena appeared amused by the defensive speech, which only irritated Victoria.

"The last thing I'm going to do is race out on the street and grab the first impoverished-looking person and make friends with him just so I can go around saying I have a poor friend. I don't choose anyone by his bank balance, whether it's large or small," she finished.

"Are you through? Should I applaud?" her mother teased.

"In another minute you are going to get this salad in your lap if you keep that up," Victoria threatened and pushed the plate away. "I'm not hungry."

"You are taking all this too seriously. You shouldn't let someone like Dirk Ramsey upset you."

"Someone like Dirk Ramsey?" A silver light danced wickedly in her gray eyes.

"Now you have me doing it!" her mother laughed ruefully. "Dirk Ramsey is just going to be another guest who will spend a couple of weeks with us—nothing more."

"I'll never believe that," Victoria stated, her mouth straightening grimly. "Dad has invited an enemy into our midst. And I'm going on the basis that to be forewarned is to be forearmed." She picked up her iced-tea glass and swirled the ice cubes. "When will our 'guest' be descending on us? In June, you said?"

"He'll arrive the second weekend in June, whatever that date is, and be there for the Lilac Festival," she explained. "You and I and Penny will fly up the middle of next week to open the house. Your father will join us that weekend."

"At least we'll have some peace and quiet before the enemy arrives," Victoria murmured caustically and sipped at her tea.

"Did you see Mrs. Ogden?" She was an elderly woman that Victoria regularly visited as a volunteer for the shut-ins.

Victoria eyed her youthful-looking mother over the rim of the glass. "Changing the subject, mom?" she challenged.

"Yes," was the emphatic response and Victoria laughed, a throaty cultured sound.

CHAPTER TWO

THE JUNE SUN had shifted its angle to glare in Victoria's eyes. She flipped the sunglasses resting on the top of her wheat-brown hair down to perch on the bridge of her nose and continued reading the novel in her hand. Her skin glistened from the liberal application of suntan lotion on all the flesh exposed to the sun's rays. The skimpy blue bikini exposed a great deal. Victoria rarely wore it in public, restricting its use mainly to sunning on the private terrace of their Mackinac Island home.

It was an old, solid-looking house, built of brick, stucco, and wood in the traditional Tudor style popular in the twenties. The terrace where Victoria was sunning was reached by a breezeway porch accessible from the living room of the house by sliding glass doors or from the front entry porch by means of a pair of iron gates. Directly behind Victoria was a garage, built in anticipation of personal motorized vehicles being brought to the island, an expectation that was never fulfilled. Transportation on the island was limited to horse and buggy, bicycles or walking. There was an airstrip where small planes landed, but as there was no bridge to the mainland, boat service ferried most of the island visitors to and from the island.

Few people ever objected to the absence of cars, since it was part of the island's charm. Those who did bemoan the fact were usually those with blisters on their heels. Everyone else simply enjoyed the leisurely pace of life on the island. And the garage of the Beaumont summer home became a storage shed for lawn tools and bicycles.

The sliding glass doors connecting the breezeway and terrace to the living room were opened. Victoria's sideways glance encompassed the angular build of Josie Largent, the Beaumont's French-speaking housekeeper for some twenty-odd years. But it was the tall, frosty glass on the tray that made Victoria straighten in the lounge chair and push the spaghetti-thin straps of her bikini into place on her shoulders.

"Lemonade! Josie, you are an angel!" she declared. *"Merci."*

"I thought you would be thirsty from all this sun," the housekeeper replied in French. Her English was flawless, but she rarely spoke it. Victoria suspected the woman believed it added distinction to her person if she spoke French. For Victoria it had meant her French language courses in school had been a snap, since she had conversed with Josie in that language from the time she was a child.

Josie held the tray out to her so Victoria could take the glass. Her sharp hazel eyes swept the bareness of Victoria's body, then flicked in the direction of the early afternoon sun.

"Do not stay in the sun too long or you will look like a lobster," she admonished, still in French. "And be careful of those sunglasses or you will have rings around your eyes like a raccoon."

"Oui, mais je ne suis pas l'enfant," Victoria sighed the protest that she wasn't a child, although she smiled affectionately when she did.

"Non?" The haughty one-word challenge was Josie's only response as she pivoted and walked under the shade of the breezeway to the glass doors.

Shaking her head wryly, Victoria took a swallow of the tart, cold liquid. Josie always managed to have the last word in any discussion. At times it was an irritating trait, but no one really minded. She was a member of the family, practically a second mother to Victoria and her sister, and much sterner with them than their parents were. Holding her glass, Victoria leaned back in the cushioned lounger and tried to find her place on the page of the book.

"There you are, Tory! I'm going to use your ten-speed. My bike has a flat tire." The greeting and announcement came out in a rush as Penny Beaumont burst onto the terrace. A silken curtain of long, honey-blond hair hung almost to her waist. Wand-slim, she was always irritated by the fact that her figure hadn't achieved the attractive curves Victoria possessed. She was sixteen and anxious to look it. Bouncing forward in a pair of denim shorts and a red T-shirt, she spied the glass Victoria held. "Lemonade?" Water had condensed on the sides of the glass. It was too wet to hang onto, and it slipped out of Victoria's fingers when Penny took it from her. She drank a third of it.

"What happened to 'May I have a drink please'?" In irritation, Victoria attempted to remind her sister of her manners.

Penny shrugged diffidently. "You would have said I could so I saved all that time and breath. It was good." She returned the glass of lemonade to Victoria.

"Thank you—you're welcome, Penny," Victoria mocked.

"I loathe that name. It's perfectly awful, and Penelope is worse." She made a face at that, and rested a hip against the edge of the redwood table. "I have decided that from now on I'm going to use my middle name. Laurel has a much better ring to it, don't you think?" she declared in a pseudo-adult air.

"Oh, yes," Victoria agreed, trying desperately not to smile. She remembered, not so many years ago; when she had disliked her own name. Now, she was simply grateful that she had never been tagged with the nickname of Vicky. "Although you didn't exactly ask my permission, yes, you may use my bike. Where are you going?"

"I'm meeting Tracy," Penny referred to one of her friends. "Then we're cycling to the dock to watch the people."

"Inspect the latest arrival of boys, don't you mean?" Victoria teased.

"That, too," Penny grinned. "You should come along. You might find someone."

"I'm not exactly on the shelf at twenty-three." Victoria murmured dryly and settled more comfortably on the lounger. Shrugging she added, "Let him find me."

Penny clicked her tongue. "You aren't supposed to wait for your ship to come in. You are supposed to swim out to meet it."

"You swim. I'll sun," she replied with unconcern.

"Suit yourself," Penny shrugged and moved in the direction of the garage. "But you're not getting any younger."

"Thank heaven," Victoria murmured to herself. She didn't want to go through those traumatic teen years again. "Have fun boy watching, Penny."

"Laurel! The name is Laurel," was the quick retort.

"Have fun . . . Laurel," Victoria stressed it with faint mockery.

Returning her attention to the open book in her hand, she half listened to the sounds of her younger sister wheeling the bike out of the garage. In a few minutes she was pedaling away from the house, and once again Victoria was alone on the terrace—but not for long. She had barely read the next paragraph when she heard her father calling for her.

"Tory? Where are you?" His voice came from inside the house.

"Out here, dad!" she called back and laid the book face down on her lap, sighing faintly at the interruption.

Sliding open the glass door, Charles Beaumont stepped into the breezeway. Although fifty-five years old, he was still a virilely handsome man. His hair had turned a distinguished iron gray and had begun to thin slightly at the temples. Age had thickened his waistline, but he had retained a physically fit look about him. His suntan was returning, although his legs beneath the tennis shorts were still a little pale. He looked healthy and there was a contented light in his blue eyes.

"Do you want something, dad?" She smiled at the sight of him.

"Were you planning on going anywhere this afternoon?" he inquired returning her smile with equal warmth.

"The only plan I have today is to get some sun and finish this book." She lifted the open novel on her lap. "Why?"

"Your mother and I are off to play a couple of games of tennis," he explained. "Dirk Ramsey said he would arrive sometime late this afternoon or early evening. We should be back by four o'clock, but in case he comes before we return, would you make our apologies to him and show him which room he'll be in? Just generally make him comfortable."

Her mouth thinned into a hard smile. "Shall I show him where we keep the family skeleton, too? Or maybe I'll unearth Penny's diary and offer it to him."

"Victoria." He murmured her name in a sigh that said they had been over all this, which indeed they had—many times.

"Oh, don't worry," she flashed in frowning irritation. "I will behave with the utmost decorum."

"That almost worries me more than if you told him off," her father replied dryly.

"Don't tempt me," Victoria murmured and opened the book to resume her reading.

Her father turned to leave. "We'll be back by four."

"Don't be late," she called the warning.

He just smiled and waved. "Hold the fort while we're gone."

Victoria watched him disappear into the house, her gray eyes dark and turbulent. "How can I hold the fort when I'm supposed to let the enemy in?" she challenged. But he was out of hearing and didn't respond.

A few minutes later, the clip-clop of hooves sounded the arrival of the horse-drawn taxi and the departure of her parents. The mere mention of Dirk Ramsey disturbed Victoria's concentration. She had to read the page she was on twice before she finally began following the novel's plot.

An hour later she moved out of the sun into the shade of the breezeway. Her skin tanned quickly and easily and Victoria chose not to flirt with the danger of a sunburn. Besides, the glare of the sun on the white pages of the book had begun to hurt her eyes, despite the sunglasses she wore. By now Victoria was too engrossed in the characters to put it down.

She was two chapters from the end when she heard the horse and carriage stop in front of the house. She glanced once toward the sun, but couldn't judge the time by its angle. There was a fleeting recognition of relief that her parents were back and she wouldn't have to be concerned about entertaining Dirk Ramsey in their absence, since he hadn't arrived. Then her concentration was back on the pages of the novel.

The horse pulling the carriage trotted away from the house at about the same time that Victoria heard the doorbell ring. It jolted along her nerve ends like an electric shock. She looked to the sliding glass doors, her eyes wary with suspicion.

Within seconds, Josie appeared and stepped onto the breezeway to announce, *"M'sieur Ramsey est arrivé."*

"Oh, no," Victoria protested in a moan, rolling her eyes heavenward. She closed the book with a snap and swung her bare legs to the stone floor. "What time is it?"

"Il est trois—"

"Only three o'clock!" she exclaimed in a mixture of anger and exasperation. "Damn him!"

"Pardon, il—"

"Dammit, Josie, speak English!" Victoria flared. She didn't want to waste time translating the housekeeper's sentences into English in her head. There were too many things to think about. Number one was the fact that she hadn't bothered to bring a beach jacket onto the terrace with her. "Where is he now?" she demanded.

"In the foyer," the housekeeper replied.

"Show him to the library," she said with quick decision. An impish part of her wanted to meet Dirk Ramsey dressed exactly as she was—which was scandalously—and play the decadent, fun-loving daughter he probably expected her to be. Victoria didn't doubt that she could carry it off, but there was her father to consider. He might see the humor in her act, but she doubted that he would be amused. "I'll use the rear service stairs to slip upstairs to my room and change." Victoria rose from the lounger and impatiently motioned the woman into the house. "Go! And, for heaven's sake, don't speak French to the man. The last thing we need is for him to start printing that dad has a French maid. They'll start imagining Brigitte Bardot instead of—" Victoria had started to finish the comparison with "a woman who looks more like De Gaulle," and thought better of it just in time. She loved the dear woman, homely though Josie was, and didn't want to hurt her feelings.

"But—" Josie started a protest.

"Go! *Vite!*" Victoria waved her inside. "Let

me know when he's in the library so I can slip in through the living room without being seen.''

"*Oui.*" It was a snapping affirmative carrying a trace of sarcasm, because the housekeeper hadn't been permitted the last word.

While she waited the interminable minutes for Josie to return, Victoria paced back and forth in front of the sliding doors. She wouldn't have time to shower away the suntan lotion or the perspiration that had collected on her skin. She'd have to be content with a quick wash and lots of cologne. What to wear? It had to be something simple and understated. That blue halter-type sundress she had just purchased, Victoria decided. With it she could wear the chunky ivory bracelets and the matching ivory pendant earrings.

With her every move planned and thought out beforehand, Victoria didn't waste time when Josie returned to signal that the coast was clear. She slipped soundlessly through the living room and darted up the rear stairs, down the narrow hall to the second-floor foyer of the main staircase and the bedrooms that branched off of it. In less than ten minutes, she had washed, changed into the dress, slipped on the jewelry, and had run a brush through her hair.

This time Victoria used the curving staircase. The grandfather clock in the corner niche of the staircase chimed a quarter past the hour of three. At the bottom of the steps her glance slid over the leather luggage on the floor. Turning, Victoria walked swiftly to the library door and paused to take a breath. One thing the expensive schools had taught her was a shatterproof composure. Victoria knew it was going to be tested. For her father's sake she was going to be pleasant even if it killed her.

Opening the door she swept into the room. "I'm sorry to have kept you waiting, Mr. Ramsey," she greeted her opponent with a smooth apology.

The man standing at the bay window turned. Victoria had her first real look at him and realized neither the photograph heading his column nor the appearance on television did him justice. Over six feet with solid flesh covering male sinew and bone, he was stunningly handsome. His hair was as black as a moonless night and cut in one of those carelessly natural styles that suggested it had just been rumpled by feminine fingers. Broad shoulders and narrow hips flaunted his bold masculinity that was almost primitive in its force.

He possessed the sun-browned features of a playboy, not someone who spent hours at a typewriter. The liquid sheen of his dark eyes reminded Victoria of the mirrored surface of a pool that didn't reveal the dangers beneath the surface. There was a cool arrogance to his look. Victoria felt her temper simmering. His dark gaze slowly inspected her from head to toe. She couldn't have felt more stripped and exposed if she had walked in wearing the skimpy bikini she'd had on.

A sheer thirst for revenge made her return the insolent appraisal. Her glittering gray eyes ran over the white shirt with its sleeves rolled partway up his forearms and the dark slacks that accented the length of his legs. When her gaze returned to his face there was something faintly taunting in his eyes, as if he was challenging her to admit she liked what she saw.

"You must be Victoria Beaumont." His voice was deep and resonant carrying a trace of contempt.

That well-taught poise came to her rescue, forcing a throaty laugh. "Is that good or bad?" she challenged and walked forward, offering her hand to him. Victoria knew she would dearly love to rake her long fingernails over his strong jaw, but she also knew she wouldn't do it. "Welcome to Mackinac Island. We weren't expecting you until later in the day so I must apologize for the absence of my parents. They are off playing tennis and won't be back until four."

"I hope my early arrival hasn't greatly inconvenienced you." He, too, was mouthing polite phrases that he didn't mean.

Even the clasp of his hand in greeting was cool, yet firm. At the contact, something quivered along her nerves—a sexual response that Victoria hadn't expected. She had thought her active dislike of a man would override his obvious male attraction. That wasn't the case. She smoothly withdrew her hand from his strong fingers.

"Not at all, Mr. Ramsey," she assured him. "Is this your first visit to Mackinac Island?" Up close she noticed there was a faintly ruthless quality to the firmness of his mouth.

"Yes." He appeared amused by her continued pursuit of polite topics. "I had a fairly good view of it from the air before we landed."

"Oh, you flew?" Victoria attempted an interested smile.

"That's generally the way you see something from the air, isn't it, Miss Beaumont?" Dirk Ramsey mocked the absurdity of her question.

"I had forgotten that you deal in words, the precise use of them. You'll simply have to forgive me for not having a better command of the language." She widened her gray eyes with obviously false innocence.

"My, my, I don't understand how you could have forgotten my profession." His amusement was openly derisive.

Victoria turned away. If she hadn't, she would have slapped his arrogant face. "My father is always entertaining friends, clients, associates, just about anybody." She put faint stress on the last to indicate Dirk Ramsey was not in any way special. "I can't be expected to

remember them all." She flashed him an over-
the-shoulder look, knowing she sounded like
some spoiled socialite and not caring.

His dark eyes had narrowed fractionally as if
he was trying to judge how much of what he saw
was real and how much was an act. A corner of
his mouth twitched, a vague signal that he'd
made his decision . . . whatever it was.

"That's asking too much, I'm sure," he
agreed with a mocking quirk of an eyebrow.
"Although you did defy all the feminine rules by
changing out of your bikini in record time, or are
you wearing it beneath that dress?"

Victoria faced him with astonishment, trying
to mask it with her poise. "How did you ferret
out that information?" She smiled but it didn't
reach the flint-gray of her eyes. "I have heard
you journalists are renowned for your sources,
but—"

"I've trained myself to be observant," Dirk
Ramsey conceded. "But the sight of a delectable
female lazing about with some triangular
patches for clothing would have attracted any
man's gaze."

"Then you saw me," she murmured stiffly.

"Those gates are only made of iron rods.
They didn't exactly block my view." His gaze
flicked her with a knowing regard for what was
beneath the dress.

Victoria filed the information away for future
use. "You can understand why I wasn't able to

greet you immediately. It would hardly have been proper to meet you in such attire, would it?'' she countered smoothly.

"Let's just say that if you had I probably would have been thinking some very improper thoughts.'' The inflection of his rich voice was deliberately evocative. He nonchalantly lessened the distance between them, his dark eyes holding her look. "What are you, the advance guard?''

"I don't think I know what you're talking about.'' Victoria tried to retain a pleasant tone although all her senses were becoming increasingly wary of his nearness.

"Was this all designed to soften me up?'' Dirk continued to regard her with a velvet quality. "All these dangerous curves and —'' his sunbrowned fingers traced the line of her bare shoulder "—soft shoulders.''

His feather-light touch unleashed an avalanche of sensual goose bumps scattering over her skin. Victoria wasn't given an opportunity to elude his hand as it was taken away as effortlessly as it had come. Again the fathomless dark eyes were roaming over her face. It was expressionless. Victoria knew that, but inside she was a caldron of hot reaction.

"I don't know why you should need softening up, Mr. Ramsey,'' she lied, since that was the whole purpose of the invitation. "But my greeting you was hardly by design.'' She kept her voice light and vaguely amused, but it was an effort. "You are the one who arrived early. In another hour, less now, my parents would have welcomed you instead of me. You and I probably wouldn't have met until dinner.''

"True," he agreed, but on a skeptical note.

Victoria wanted the subject changed—and quickly. She didn't trust her temper to continue to assure him that he was welcome in this house.

"Did our housekeeper offer you some refreshments? Perhaps you'd like a cold drink after your trip," she suggested like a dutiful hostess.

"I prefer coffee . . . if you'll have some with me," Dirk countered.

Hot coffee when she was already steaming? "Of course," Victoria agreed and walked to the door. "Josie?" The housekeeper was in the hallway practically before Victoria got her name out. Victoria didn't even have to step out of the doorway.

"Oui?" the housekeeper responded.

"Deux café au lait avec sucre." Her request was automatically issued in French.

"Café noir pour moi." Dirk Ramsey refused milk and sugar for his coffee in flawless French.

Victoria pivoted in surprise and recovered immediately. "You speak French very well, Mr. Ramsey."

"Why is it that your compliment gives me the impression of an accusation?" he asked in a vaguely drawling challenge.

Remembering the housekeeper, Victoria glanced over her shoulder to find Josie still standing in the hall. "That's all, Josie," she dismissed the woman before responding to his question. "I can't imagine why you would think my remark would be an accusation."

"Maybe because you regard me as uncouth and unprincipled, and generally a little beneath you," he suggested.

She hadn't realized her dislike was so apparent. "Really?" Victoria laughed a shade maliciously. "I thought that was the way you were regarding me, Mr. Ramsey."

"Be assured, no one could ever accuse you of being uncouth." Thick, spiky lashes came down to hood his look. "You are polished and refined to impeccable perfection. Forgive me if I keep looking for the flaws of human failing."

"And have you found any?" She had to bite her tongue to keep from mentioning a few of his.

"Only that slip of superiority when you addressed your housekeeper in French."

"Did that sound superior?" Victoria murmured. "I have been conversing with Josie in French since I was a toddler. So perhaps I can be forgiven for that," she suggested with cloying sweetness.

"She's the treasured family retainer, I take it," he mocked.

"Every aristocratic family has one, don't they?" The retort was out before Victoria could stop it, smugly taunting with an acid bite. She turned swiftly to distract his attention. "Did you have an opportunity to look over the books? My father has an extensive collection." She waved to the bookshelves. "Naturally, you are welcome to read any of them while you are here. We never have a shortage of reading material."

"It is an impressive number of books. Most people couldn't afford to own a tenth of them," he commented and it sounded like a condemnation.

Victoria was about to lash out at him when Josie knocked at the library door and entered with the coffee. The timing was excellent because Victoria feared she would have lost her temper otherwise.

CHAPTER THREE

THE SHEEN of those black eyes was making Victoria increasingly uncomfortable. There had been no more baiting comments from Dirk Ramsey while they drank their coffee, but that aloof derision tinged with amusement rarely left his features. When Victoria had exhausted her supply of safe small talk, she had to find something else to occupy him.

"Would you like to see your room?" she suggested. "I'm sure you will want to unpack and settle in before dinner."

"Yes, that would be a good idea," he agreed smoothly.

Yet Victoria had the distinct impression that he knew how eager she was to escape his company. It was becoming more and more difficult to keep a rein on her temper. Unless she was mistaken, he seemed to know it and regarded her facade of pleasantry with arrogant amusement.

Rising from the leather-cushioned chair, Victoria set her cup on the tray and walked to the door. Dirk Ramsey was there first to open it for her, his show of manners as much a mockery as hers.

"I'll get my luggage," he announced when they reached the foyer. His suitcases weren't sitting where they had been. He arched a questioning eyebrow at Victoria. "Someone must have carried them upstairs already."

"It must have been Josie." Victoria shrugged in unconcern and started up the stairs.

"They were heavy," Dirk replied with a suggestion of protest.

"Josie is strong," she assured him that it wasn't unusual.

He started up the stairs behind her. "Comes from good peasant stock, I suppose," he offered dryly.

Victoria hesitated on the stairs, her anger flaring out of control for a short instant. She managed to contain all but a small thread of it that laced her attempted light reply, "I don't think my parents checked her bloodlines before they hired her twenty-some years ago."

"An oversight, no doubt."

Her long nails dug into the sensitive palms of her hands. Victoria laughed. It was either that or shriek at him. "You have such a droll sense of humor, Mr. Ramsey."

"I do?" He eyed her with suspicion.

"Oh, yes. I read a couple of your columns. They were absolutely hilarious!" she declared. "You really should write comedies. I think you would be very good at it."

"You thought they were funny?" Dirk repeated. His dry tone indicated he didn't believe her.

"Especially when you said all that nonsense about my father. It was priceless." Victoria flashed him a wide smile and continued up the steps. "The guest bedroom has its own private bath and a small sitting area. I hope you find it comfortable." Victoria wished there was a bedroom in the attic where she could put him.

At the head of the stairs she turned right into the foyer and walked to the door at its widest point. She entered the room ahead of Dirk Ramsey, sidestepping the luggage stacked inside the door.

It was a simple room with dormer windows letting in light. The walnut bed was covered with a tangerine-colored spread. The same color was repeated in the plaid material of a stuffed armchair and in the curtains at the windows. A small desk and chair sat beneath one of the windows.

Crossing the room Victoria opened a door. "Here is your bathroom." She waved to another set of doors. "There are the closets with plenty of hangers for your clothes." She continued her sweep of the room. "Of course, you have a dresser, too." Finally she stopped by the bed. "I doubt if you'll need them, but there are extra blankets on the top shelf of the closet."

All the while she had been showing him the room, Dirk Ramsey had remained just inside the door. Now that she was finished he made no response and bent instead to his luggage. He picked up a gray metal case and carried it to the desk where he opened it.

"My typewriter seems to have survived the trip," he murmured.

"You are on vacation, aren't you?" Victoria

sat on the bed, putting her hands behind her and leaning on them. "You surely aren't planning to work while you're here."

"I'm always working." Dirk slanted her a smile as he closed the case. "But to answer your question, theoretically I'm on vacation. If I find enough material I'll do a couple of columns while I'm here. I like to stay ahead of my deadlines."

"I'm certain you'll find enough material for some columns while you are with us. After all, with your imagination it doesn't take much." Victoria gave him a wide-eyed look. "All you need is a few facts and you can embroider the rest."

When he turned to move leisurely across the room to where she was sitting, Victoria thought she saw his tongue running along the inside of his cheek. She had the impression her supposedly innocent gibe had irritated him just a little, and she was glad.

"How do you like the room?" she inquired to fill the suddenly tense silence.

"Very nice." But his dark eyes never let their attention wander from her face. When he stopped he was towering at the foot of the bed, his arms crossed to stretch the material of his shirt across the muscled width of his chest. "You look very natural sitting on that bed," Dirk observed. "Are you part of the furnishings? Something to keep me warm at night so I don't have to use those blankets in the closet?"

Indignation burned her face. Victoria didn't

waste any time pushing off the bed. All the while she was mentally counting to ten and beyond. She had succeeded in holding her temper to this point. Victoria didn't want to ruin it all by losing it now. His suggestion that she might sleep with him had robbed her of speech anyhow, as well as the thought of being nestled against his naked, male chest.

"I think that was uncalled-for," Victoria finally managed to murmur tautly.

The door beckoned with an escape route and Victoria ordered her legs to take it. Averting her gaze from his compelling face she moved away from the bed, taking the short, straight-line route to the door. It meant walking past him, but she didn't expect Dirk to stop her.

When she was level with him, an arm came out to cross in front of her and hook a hand on the side of her waist. Victoria took an instant step backward to avoid the hard biceps that had flexed against her breasts. His hand stayed on her waist, his fingers firm in their spreading clasp. His touch started miniature tremors in her stomach to confuse her.

"You're right." His voice was low and almost reluctant in its admission. Victoria was surprised he admitted it at all and lifted her gaze to his incredibly handsome face. Immediately she felt drawn by the mysterious blackness of his eyes. The dangerous enchantment made her heart beat faster. "I was fantasizing about how enjoyable it could be to have you for a sleeping companion.

Something a proper guest wouldn't admit, but I could hardly be described as proper."

Wicked, perhaps, Victoria thought. A dangerous temptation seemed to charge the air. But she wasn't about to flirt with the enemy, especially when she wasn't sufficiently armed to combat his potent weaponry.

"If you'll excuse me." Victoria glanced pointedly at the hand on her waist that was detaining her. When she lifted her gaze she let it dwell on him with haughty disdain, although that was far from the mixed-up emotions quivering inside.

As his hand came away his arm made a sweeping gesture to offer clear passage. His courtly manner was rife with mockery and Victoria's agitation quickly turned to anger. It was evident in every controlled line of her carriage as she moved to the door. His low chuckle laughed at her when she carefully closed it behind her, rather than slam it as her temper wanted her to do.

Her teeth were clenched in pure rage. She would have stormed down the stairs except the high heels of her sandals forced her to take the steps at a slower pace. When Victoria reached the foyer Josie appeared and asked a question in French, but Victoria's mind was seething with too many angry thoughts to translate it.

"Oh, speak English!" she exclaimed in irritation.

"Is everything all right?" Josie repeated the question with stiff formality.

"No, everything isn't all right!" Victoria snapped.

"What is wrong? Isn't the room to his liking?" the housekeeper questioned sharply.

"The room is to his liking all right. It's Dirk Ramsey who isn't to my liking," she retorted.

"Do you wish—"

"I wish to have him out of here!" Victoria interrupted.

"Mr. Ramsey is your father's guest," Josie reminded her.

"And I mean to take that up with dad the minute he returns." She pivoted away to enter the living room.

It seemed she had to wait forever for that eventuality. The ticking of the grandfather clock in the stairwell seemed to be at an abominably slow rhythm. With each minute, Victoria's resentment of Dirk Ramsey boiled hotter and hotter. When her parents did return it was bubbling over.

The carefree sounds of their laughing voices as they entered the house only added fuel to her anger. Her hands were clenched into rigid fists at her sides that they should sound so happy when she had been through such a trying ordeal.

Carrying their tennis rackets they strolled into the living room their hands linked together. Her mother looked youthful and smart in her white tennis skirt, a radiant flush to her cheeks as she looked into the smiling face of the man at her side. The clock chimed four times to mark the hour.

"It's about time you came back," Victoria declared in a tight voice.

"Hello, Tory." Her father turned his smile to her. "Did you finish your book?"

"No! I was *rudely* interrupted by the arrival of your Dirk Ramsey." She placed sarcastic emphasis on the adverb.

"He arrived already?" Surprise replaced the smiling expression on Charles Beaumont's features.

"About an hour ago," Victoria informed him.

"I hope you made him welcome and explained why your mother and I weren't here." Unlinking his fingers from his wife's hand he came farther into the room, setting his tennis racket on the sofa in front of the large stone fireplace.

Her mother followed him. "Is he in his room now?"

"Yes, he's in his room, and yes, I made him welcome." Victoria was trying very hard not to unleash her temper on them. "Yes, I explained where you were. Although he was skeptical that your absence might have been deliberate."

"Deliberate?" Her father frowned.

Victoria squared around to face him. "Ramsey thought I was the advance guard to soften him up," she said icily.

His head came back as he emitted a hearty

laugh. "You must have been very charming, Tory. I congratulate you."

"Save your congratulations!" she erupted angrily. "If you let that man stay in this house for two weeks, I'm moving out! I have had all his veiled insults that I can stand."

"Victoria," her mother attempted to soothe her ruffled feathers with a calming tone.

"Don't Victoria me. I mean it!" she flashed. "He is the most crude, objectionable man you can imagine. Arrogant, conceited, drunk on his own self-importance, he—"

"Ssh, Tory, that's enough." Her father raised a silencing hand.

"Don't you shush me! I've had to bite my tongue so many times it's sore!" Victoria declared in a stormy protest. "You are wasting your time having that man here. Dirk Ramsey! Dirk, I bet that isn't even his real name. It's probably a nickname that he's earned from stabbing people in the back!"

"You are mistaken, Miss Beaumont," a voice drawled behind her and Victoria pivoted to see Dirk Ramsey in the living-room arch, a hand thrust negligently in the pocket of his dark slacks. "Dirk is my real name."

"It's also your real nature," she retorted. It was too late to pretend now. Victoria could tell by his hard expression that he had heard everything she had said about him.

"Tory, Mr. Ramsey is a guest in our home," her father cautioned her to hold her tongue.

But Victoria had been doing that for too long. "Mr. Ramsey is a pain in the—"

"Victoria!" Her mother's shocked voice cut across the sentence.

A smile of insolent amusement slanted the handsomely cut mouth. "A lady wouldn't use the language you were thinking, Miss Beaumont," Dirk taunted.

"Since you view everything from the gutter, I thought it was the only kind you would understand!" she retorted.

"Victoria, you will apoligize at once!" her father demanded in cold anger.

"No, there's no need for her to apologize," Dirk insisted and moved into the room. "I much prefer her honest hostility to the false welcome I received earlier." He stopped in front of her, his dark enigmatic eyes studying the pride and temper animating her classic features.

Her father came up behind her and put an arm on her shoulders. "I'm sorry, Mr. Ramsey. I'm afraid my daughter is—"

"Is commendably loyal to you," Dirk interrupted to complete the sentence, his gaze finally swinging from Victoria to her father. "I wouldn't apoligize for that, Mr. Beaumont. It should be a source of pride to you that she feels so protective and defensive on your behalf."

"It's generous of you to be so understanding. Thank you." Charles Beaumont offered his hand and Dirk shook it firmly.

"Getting better acquainted is the purpose of

my visit," he said. "There aren't many parents who inspire such a fierce loyalty in their children, so I suppose we have already begun to fulfill that purpose." Releasing her father's hand, Dirk returned his attention to Victoria who was still eyeing him with hostility. "Now that your daughter has aired her animosity and everything is out in the open, I think we can observe a truce for the rest of my stay."

"With you, I'm sure it will be an 'armed' truce, Mr. Ramsey," Victoria responded to his half challenge.

"Call me Dirk . . . that way you can pretend you are stabbing me every time you say my name," he smiled lazily and offered his hand to her. "And I'll call you Victoria and think of the queen. Maybe I'll remember to be properly humble in your presence."

She placed her hand in his and gave him an arching smile. "That I would like to see . . . Dirk." And she stabbed him with his name.

Instead of grasping her hand to shake it, he gripped her fingers and bent over her hand. When Victoria realized his intention she automatically tightened her fingers to withdraw her hand from his descending mouth. But it was too late to avoid the warm lips that pressed themselves to the back of her hand in a continental gesture that he carried off with a suave ease. The contact ignited a liquid fire that coursed through her veins.

As he straightened, there was a devilish blackness to his eyes. When he released her hand it was all Victoria could do to keep from rubbing the place where his lips had been, wanting to erase their imprint and the tingling sensation that remained.

She did the next best thing by mocking the gesture. "such gallantry! However did you acquire such finesse?" she taunted.

"By watching Errol Flynn movies," Dirk responded in the same vein. Then he was turning away. "You haven't introduced me to your wife, Beaumont."

"I beg your pardon," her father apologized and reached out to draw his wife forward. "Lena, I would like you to officially meet Dirk Ramsey. My wife, and friend, Lena Beaumont."

"I'm sorry our meeting couldn't have been in friendlier circumstances, Mr. Ramsey," her mother apologized as she shook his hand.

"Don't let it trouble you," Dirk smiled and Victoria saw how devastatingly good-looking he could be when his features weren't tainted with cynicism. "I'm pleased to meet you at last, Mrs. Beaumont. I have often heard you described as your husband's most valuable asset. Perhaps it's a description that isn't so far off the mark."

"Thank you." Her mother accepted the compliment with genuine modesty. "I do hope you'll find these next two weeks with us both enjoyable and informative."

"I am certain I will." Just for an instant his gaze flicked to Victoria as if she might contribute to it.

But her mother claimed his attention again. "Would you excuse me while I go change?" she requested politely and glanced at her husband. "Why don't you fix Mr. Ramsey a drink? I don't think it's too early for a predinner cocktail."

"Excellent idea, dear," he agreed as she smiled and moved toward the foyer. "What would you like, Dirk? A martini?"

"I don't drink, thank you. Fix one for yourself if you like," he insisted.

"Don't tell me you don't possess any vices . . . Dirk?" Victoria couldn't help gibing.

"One or two." His gaze ran suggestively over her figure to let her know what one of them was.

For a moment she felt out of her league. "Excuse me. I have a book to finish." She considered her retreat to the breezeway to be a strategic one.

The breezeway didn't offer total seclusion. Neither did the book offer escape. The voices of the two men in the living room drifted through the glass doors to distract her attention. Victoria found herself listening to their apparently amicable discussion. She envied her father's ability to respond so naturally and without any defensiveness to the questions Dirk put to him. The questions were casual, containing nothing controversial, and his tone indicated an appropriate interest in the answers.

The glass door to the breezeway slid open.

"Would we disturb you too much if we joined you out here, Tory?" her father asked. "It's too nice out here to stay inside."

"No, not at all." Her sigh revealed the novel's inability to recapture her attention, but she kept it propped in front of her so she wouldn't be expected to join in their conversation.

Her gaze wandered from the pages of the book when Dirk walked by her, but he appeared indifferent to her presence. She was glad, she told herself.

"Do you play tennis, Dirk?" her father asked.

"Yes, when I can find a partner, which isn't always easy if you are in a strange city."

"You do quite a bit of lecturing, don't you?" her father remembered, which was something Victoria hadn't known.

"Yes," he admitted, but no more than that.

Charles Beaumont didn't pursue that topic and returned instead to the first. "We'll play some tennis tomorrow. A couple of matches of mixed doubles. Tory plays a good game of tennis. She can be your partner."

"Thanks for volunteering me, dad," she said caustically. "Maybe I have other plans."

Her father grinned. "But you don't, do you?" When no reply was immediately forthcoming, he laughed. "That's what I thought."

"I think she's worried that if she plays as my partner in tennis it might become habit-forming," Dirk suggested with a baiting look. "She doesn't want to be accused of siding with the enemy."

"But we have an armed truce, remember?" Victoria offered with a honeyed smile.

"I remember," he assured her. "I was wondering if you did." The long, lazy look he gave her was subtly seductive. She felt it tugging at her breath, trying to steal it and almost succeeding. Her sister, Penny, chose that moment to return and distract everyone's attention.

"My youngest," Charles identified her as Penny stepped off the ten-speed bike and parked it alongside the garage on the terrace. Her waist-length blond hair swung like a rippling curtain of silk when she walked toward them. Her blue eyes focused on Dirk with open speculation and interest. "Dirk, I'd like you to meet my daughter—"

"Laurel," Penny quickly supplied. At the raised eyebrow from her father, she explained. "My name is actually Penelope, but my friends call me Laurel."

"I'm pleased to meet you, Laurel." He shook her hand, holding it a little longer than Victoria thought was necssary.

"You must be Dirk Ramsey." There was a dazed look to Penny's blue eyes. "You are much better looking in person than those pictures I've seen in the papers."

"Flattery will get you anything, Laurel." To prove it, Dirk gave the susceptible teenager a dazzling smile. Victoria could almost see Penny melting. There wasn't any way she could provide her sister some immunity against Dirk's particular brand of sexual magnetism. Heavens, she didn't even possess it herself!

CHAPTER FOUR

VICTORIA PARTNERED Dirk Ramsey in tennis the
following afternoon. They lost the first match,
in great part due to her lack of concentration. It
wasn't easy to ignore the vital, sun-browned
man sharing the court with her or to forget the
conflicting emotions he generated.

Each time the resonant timbre of his voice
called for the ball or absently complimented her
on a good serve or a good return, her attention
was diverted from the blistering pace of the
game. She was more conscious of where Dirk
was on the court than where the ball was.

It wasn't until the middle of the second match
that she began to play with her usual skill and
concentration, subconsciously accepting him as
her teammate and letting her constant awareness
of his position on the court become an advantage rather than a diversion. They began scoring
more points than they lost, drawing even. Victoria became caught up in the exhilaration of
competing.

When it was her return that scored the match
point, she forgot everything but the elation of
winning. Her parents approached the net to
acknowledge their loss and Victoria went forward to accept their congratulations with Dirk at

her side. She glanced at him with a winded smile that shared the victory. She was conscious of the masculine arm that curved around the back of her waist. The contact was pleasantly exciting rather than annoying.

"Great game, Tory." Her mother reached across the net to shake her hand. "You, too, Dirk."

"That last point was a dandy, Tory," her father declared a little out of breath. "You put the ball at my feet. I didn't have a chance to get my racket on it. And remind me never to play singles with your partner. He'd wipe me off the court." He laughed and shook hands with Dirk who had shifted his racket to the hand on Victoria's waist.

"I doubt if it would ever be easy to beat you, Chuck," Dirk insisted.

A light gleamed in her father's eye as he gently mocked, "Now who is courting whose favor?"

A low yet hearty laugh came from Dirk. It turned Victoria's head, lifting it so she could see his face beneath the white visor she wore. Her senses quivered to a finely honed alertness, attuned to the male vigor of the man beside her.

The white of his shirt contrasted sharply with his tanned skin, glistening like polished bronze from the sheen of perspiration. That dampness coiled the dark curling hairs visible at the V front of his shirt even tighter, while it intensified the warm, earthy smell of him that stimulated her already quickly beating heart. The nerve ends in her shoulder began to tingle with its easy contact with his solid chest, rising and falling in a comfortable rhythm despite the exertion of the tennis match.

Her lips felt dry and Victoria pressed them together to moisten them with her tongue. She could taste the salty tang of her own perspiration and felt the dampness of her own hair curling against the sides of her face. As if feeling her eyes on him, Dirk turned his head to look down at her upturned face.

The heady male smile remained grooved into his tanned cheeks, but the laughing glint in his coal-black eyes took on another dimension. His gaze shifted to dwell on the moistness of her lips. The sensual impact of his look struck Victoria low in her midsection and spread to attack her legs with a giddy weakness. Instantly Victoria realized that she had let herself drift under the spell of his dangerously handsome looks and potent charm.

With a quick turn of her head she broke free of the spell, feeling more out of breath than when the match had ended. "Let's call it quits for today and play the tie breaker some other time," Victoria suggested.

"I second that," her mother agreed.

There was nothing restrictive in the touch of the male hand resting on the back of her waist. All Victoria had to do was simply turn and walk away from it. She did, moving parallel with the net to the end pole and walking around it to the gate in the tennis fence. Naturally Dirk followed but so did her parents.

Before leaving the court, they picked up the protective covers for their rackets and the small leather satchels. Outside the gate the quartet continued to the benches where they stopped by a silent, mutual consent.

As Victoria unzipped her bag and took out a hand towel, she couldn't make up her mind whether it was by accident or design that she and Dirk were separated from her parents by several feet. She rubbed her face dry with the terry cloth towel and tried to ignore him.

"Your father plays a great game," Dirk commented, tipping his head back to wipe the perspiration from his throat.

Victoria flashed him a wary look. "And he doesn't cheat, either."

His hand halted the towel at the base of his throat as he turned to level his gaze at her. "I don't recall ever suggesting that he did."

"You have made other malicious interpretations of his accomplishments so I have no cause to think you wouldn't do it now," she retorted in a low undertone.

His eyes remained harshly black, not lightened by humor although his mouth twisted into a smile. "We are supposed to be observing a truce."

"An armed truce," Victoria reminded him, and flipped her visor to jam it in the satchel.

"Hello, Dirk." Penny approached him at a sedate walk instead of her usual madcap run. In fact, Victoria thought she almost sauntered over to him. She had the impression her little sister had matured overnight.

"Hello, Laurel." Dirk returned the greeting with a gentleness that was indulgent, as if he knew what was happening to the girl. Victoria knew, too. Penny was in the throes of her first adult infatuation.

"I saw you playing and stopped to watch," Penny said to explain her presence. "You have a wicked backhand. Maybe you could give me some pointers sometime."

"How about right now?" Dirk suggested.

"I—" Penny's delight nearly bubbled over into teenage exuberance, but she checked it just in time, "—I'd like that."

"Let's go before someone else takes the court." He took his racket out of its cover.

"May I borrow yours, Tory?" Penny asked.

"Sure." Victoria shrugged, knowing her younger sister would never understand a refusal—or accept it.

She watched the pair take the court and observed Dirk instructing Penny how to position herself, step into the swing and follow through. It was amazing how Penny, who was such a quick learner, was so slow to catch on.

"I see Dirk is teaching Penny the finer points of the backhand," her father remarked, coming to stand beside Victoria and watch.

Victoria turned away. "She needs to learn

about a backhand all right, the kind applied to her bottom,'' she said in disgust.

"She's young,'' her mother reasoned.

"What's his excuse?'' Victoria challenged, slicing a glance at the tall, dark man on the court. "He's experienced enough to know what she's doing.'' In Victoria's opinion Penny was making a fool of herself, and she didn't like the idea of Dirk Ramsey laughing at any of her family.

"He's being kind,'' her mother insisted.

"Kind? That isn't an adjective I would associate with him,'' she retorted. "What exactly do you know about him, dad?''

"Not much,'' he admitted, pursing his lips together in a considering expression. "I know he came up the hard way.''

"The hard way, huh?'' Victoria was mockingly skeptical. "With his looks I can't imagine that anything was ever hard for him.''

"With his looks,'' her mother inserted, "I imagine it was difficult for people to take him seriously as a hard-issue journalist.''

"I'm sure you are right, Lena,'' her father agreed.

Victoria didn't, but rather than argue she excused herself. "I'm going to walk for a bit before my legs cramp up.''

AT DINNER that evening, Penny appeared at the table with her long, honey-blond hair swept on top of her head in a smooth coil. Victoria recognized the gold hooped earrings her sister was wearing as a pair of her own, obviously borrowed from her jewelry case. Her young sister was attempting to look worldly even though she lacked the experience to carry it off.

Aware that it was all done for Dirk's benefit, both Victoria and her parents were careful not to comment on Penny's sudden burst of sophistication. Only Victoria was close enough to hear Dirk voice his reaction to the new Penny.

"You are very attractive tonight. With your hair up like that you look very young and vulnerable." Which was true, even though it was the exact opposite of the effect that Penny was trying to achieve. And Penny wouldn't have believed it from anyone else. Dirk took the sting out of his comment by adding, "And I feel very old in comparison." It was the twinge of regret in his look and voice that made the difference, and soothed Penny's hurt feelings. In truth, he was more than twice Penny's age.

Victoria's reaction to his comment was mixed. On the one hand, she was glad he had been truthful and had not let Penny think she looked older. Yet she resented him, too, for gently crushing Penny's sensitive feelings. Victoria didn't like regarding Dirk with this ambivalence. This constant fluctuation was disturbing.

BREAKFAST WAS not served at a set time in the Beaumont household, especially when they were vacationing on the island. Whenever anyone came downstairs in the morning there was cereal, fruit, toast and juice in the kitchen. Victoria ate her toast and coffee alone in the breakfast nook partitioned from the kitchen by a decorative iron screen. Everyone else, with the exception of Penny who was still in bed, had already eaten.

When she had finished, she stopped by the library where her father was reading and her mother was catching up on some family correspondence. Her father glanced at her over the rims of his reading glasses.

"Good morning, Tory," he greeted her.

"Hi. I'm going into town this morning for some shampoo and things. Is there anything you wanted me to pick up for you, mom?" she asked.

"Not that I can think of, no," her mother replied after a second's pause.

"Have you phoned for a taxi or were you planning to walk?" The inquiry came from her father. The smile on his face said he had already guessed her answer.

"Call me one, will you?" Victoria grinned. "I'm going upstairs for my purse. I'll probably have lunch in town, so if I'm not back by noon don't wait for me."

"All right," her mother agreed.

Ascending the stairs Victoria took her time. Unless there was a taxi in the immediate vicinity of their summer home, it would be several minutes before one arrived since it was literally dependent on horsepower. In her room, she paused in front of the vanity mirror to adjust the mandarinlike collar of her sleeveless lavender dress. At the last minute, she added a narrow white belt to make a waistline in the straight style of the dress with its split side pleats.

Her bedroom faced the front of the house directly above the library. The bay window that jutted out from the room below was repeated in her bedroom. The lower half of one window was raised to let in the heavy scent of lilacs blooming in the front of the house. A pair of birds chattered noisily outside the window, nearly drowning out the sound of trotting hooves approaching the house.

Slipping the strap of her purse over her shoulder Victoria hurried out of the bedroom into the second-floor foyer. At the same moment Dirk came out of his bedroom.

Good manners dictated that she couldn't ignore him, so she tossed him an indifferent, "Good morning." Victoria would have left it at that, but she wasn't given the chance.

"Is that your taxi pulling up outside the house?" Dirk asked.

"Yes." She paused with a hand on the railing of the stairs. "I'm on my way into town. Why?"

Dirk stopped near her, dressed in oyster-gray slacks and a lighter gray shirt. "Would you mind if I came along with you?"

Irritated because she couldn't think of an adequate reason to refuse him, Victoria retorted, "I thought you would probably be spending this morning sharpening your pen so you could dip it in your poison ink."

He swept her cool expression with a lazy look. "I haven't obtained enough material yet. May I ride with you?"

Victoria took a deep breath and let it out in a long, exasperated sound. "Of course."

"Don't sound too overjoyed or I might get the wrong idea," he mocked.

"Would that it were true," she murmured and started down the stairs. It didn't require a sixth sense to know that her leisurely, peaceful morning in town had just been shot down by the enemy.

Her father was in the entryway when Victoria rounded the curve of the staircase. "Your taxi is waiting." When he caught sight of the man behind her, he asked, "Are you going with Tory?"

"Yes," Dirk answered without elaboration.

Her father didn't seem unduly surprised by it. "It's a beautiful morning. We'll see you when you come back." He continued on to the library.

Crossing the foyer Victoria walked to the front door. Dirk reached in front of her to open it. She inclined her head in a haughty acknowledgement of his courtesy and avoided that mocking light she knew would be in his gaze. There wasn't really any reason for her to be so stiff and formal, but it seemed her only protection.

The main entrance of the house was recessed under the timbered roof that connected the breezeway to the garage. The horse-drawn taxi waited for them by the stone walk. Dirk helped her into the rubber-wheeled buggy, then climbed in to sit beside her. Victoria didn't remember the seats being so narrow. After asking the driver to take them to the harbor, she adjusted the side pleat of her dress so it wouldn't reveal so much thigh.

With a flick of his whip and the urging click of his tongue, the driver had the horse leaning into its harness. The buggy started forward with a slight lurch before the horse settled into a steady trot.

The silence was more than Victoria could tolerate. It made her too conscious of the muscled arm and shoulder brushing against hers. She moved her purse onto her lap so it wouldn't be poking her in the side and let her fingers fidget with the metal clasp.

"What are your first impressions of Mackinac Island?" Her gray eyes slid him a sideways look of feigned interest.

"It has a certain nostalgic appeal, an escape into the past." His encompassing glance included the bobbing head of the horse pulling the taxi-buggy, and the green trees rising out of the rocky ground.

"It's certain that the pollution problems here are limited to horse droppings and litter," Victoria admitted with a wry smile.

"How long have you been coming here?" Dirk questioned.

"We've spent at least a month here every summer since I was five," she replied. The question brought back a lot of childhood memories of idyllic days on the island. "I loved the horses," Victoria recalled. "When I was seven one of my friends had her own pony and cart. I begged my father to let me have one, too, but he convinced me it wasn't fair to the pony since it would be lonely all the months I was gone."

"It must be tough to be the daughter of rich parents," he derided, a corner of his mouth quirking.

Her bristling defense was automatic. "It has its drawbacks."

"Such as?" Dirk challenged in a taunting drawl.

"Such as enduring the company of rude reporters."

Dirk chuckled. "I think the lady is trying to put me down."

"Wherever did you get that idea?" she murmured with cool innocence.

"Where did you go to college? Bryn Mawr? Vassar?"

"What makes you think I didn't go to Ann Arbor?" Victoria countered.

"Did you?" He arched a skeptical brow.

"As a matter of fact I didn't," she fairly snapped out the admission. "But I have no doubt that you already know which university I attended. More than likely you researched the background of everyone in the family, including me. I'm quite sure you are fully aware of all my vital statistics.''

''No, not all,'' Dirk denied that, a wicked light glinting in his dark eyes. ''But I think I could guess quite accurately what they are, considering what little of your body I didn't see in that swimsuit.'' His gaze made a slow and deliberately insolent sweep of her figure. ''Do you want to know what I think your measurements are?''

''Not particularly.'' Her lips thinned into an angry line as her fingers tightened protectively on the small shield of her purse.

Dirk leaned forward and asked the driver to stop for a minute. His request caught Victoria off guard, confusing her as to his motive. He stepped out and walked to a lilac bush growing close to the road. Snapping off a cluster, he returned to the buggy and dropped the richly scented flowers in her lap as he climbed back in.

''What's this for?'' Victoria frowned, wondering if it was supposed to be some kind of peace offering. She had no desire to make peace with him.

''You seem to be having trouble finding something to do with your hands,'' Dirk replied as the buggy lurched forward again. ''I thought you could play with the flower instead of your purse. At the rate you're going the clasp will be broken before we reach the harbor.''

Even as he made his explanation Victoria discovered her nervous fingers were already twirling the stem of the flower, scattering the scent in all directions to envelop them. She forced her hand to hold it still.

"Maybe if I put my arm back here, you'll feel more relaxed." He rested his arm along the back of the buggy seat. Her shoulder was no longer rubbing against it, but she could feel her hair brushing his sleeve. If anything the suggestion of having his arm around her was even more disturbing. He probably knew it, but Victoria would never admit it. "What do you do, Victoria?"

"Do? By that, do you mean am I gainfully employed?" She bridled at the question and forced a thin thread of calm into her answer. "The answer is no, I don't work at anything where I draw a salary. I'm involved in arranging a great many charity benefits and I do a lot of volunteer work at the hospital and with the elderly. I keep busy."

"All that education going to waste," he murmured in subtle condemnation.

"Education is never wasted," she defended. "I'm doing something that is both worthwhile and needed. If I had told you that I worked as a secretary or a teacher, you probably would have pointed out that someone else needed the job and its salary more than I did. You would have found fault either way."

"You're probably right," Dirk conceded, eyeing her with a considering look.

"I know I am." Victoria stared straight

ahead, her jaw clenched in an effort to check her growing anger.

"Unmarried, no engagement ring, no men friends, no lover—at least I haven't seen any evidence of one. You are a beautiful woman, Victoria, what's the matter? Are you frigid or training to become a nun?" He was deliberately baiting her and sitting back with amusement to watch the result.

"No to both! At the moment I don't happen to be dating anyone steadily. As yet I haven't found a man I want to spend a whole day with or a whole night, let alone the rest of my life! To me, marriage isn't like a dress that you throw away when you get tired of it. When I get married it's going to be for keeps. I know it would be better press if I were a jet-setter involved in a lot of scandalous affairs, but that's not me!" She glared at him with icy gray eyes. "I don't care if you consider me a freak."

"Rare, but I wouldn't say a freak." There was quiet contemplation in the steady regard of his eyes, but his reaction otherwise was unreadable.

Victoria had had enough of being on the sharp end of his pointed questions. It was time he had a taste of his own treatment.

"What about you? What makes you tick?" she challenged. "Tell me about your life!"

"It's your typical hard-luck-kid-growing-up-in-the-streets story with his mother sick in some dingy apartment," Dirk shrugged but with a harsh bite to his self-mockery. "I always worked. Sometimes the job was legal; sometimes it wasn't. Vacation to me only meant that I didn't have to go to school. I had to work at two full-time jobs to make it through city college, so I never had time to study to make the grades that might earn me a scholarship. But I got into a university and took all the courses I could on journalism, speech, and television. Eventually I obtained my degree.''

"Then what?'' Victoria prompted and refused to let herself feel any pity for him.

"I couldn't get a job. I ended up working on a weekly newspaper in a little burg outside Washington, D.C. When I wasn't setting the press or bugging the advertisers or taking want ads, I wrote articles that I started submitting to the editorial pages of big newspapers. That was the beginning of my column. So you see—'' Dirk glanced at her, a faintly sardonic expression on the handsomely carved features ''—my life story is very boring. What about yours?''

Boring? It sounded like a determined struggle to Victoria, a determined struggle by a tenacious fighter. But she doubted that her opinion would mean anything.

"Mine is just as simple. I was born with a silver spoon in my mouth and I've been collecting them ever since,'' she retorted.

Unexpectedly, Dirk laughed. Equally unexpectedly, Victoria found herself joining in.

CHAPTER FIVE

THE HORSE-DRAWN TAXI stopped at the curb by the white-fronted buildings that marked the commerical district. Dirk climbed out of the buggy first and turned to help Victoria down. She reached for his hands, but they circled her waist instead to lift her out of the buggy. Clutching the lilac in one hand, Victoria gripped the flexed muscles of his upper arms for balance. When he slowly set her on the ground, she ended up sliding the last couple of inches against his chest with his hands deliberately forcing her that close. The contact with his hard, lean body had her pulse beating wildly. Victoria quickly pushed some distance between them and thanked the driver. She hurried onto the covered sidewalk by the storefronts.

"Are you late for an appointment?" Dirk's voice taunted her haste.

Victoria pivoted, summoning her composure to come to her rescue. "No, I . . . ." She glanced to the street just as a carriage filled with tourists pulled away from the ticket office, the fringe on its top swinging with the rhythm of the trotting horses. "I was just getting out of the way of the tour carriage."

"Oh." It was a disbelieving sound, but Dirk didn't pursue her lie. "Where shall I meet you?" He joined her on the sidewalk, drawing her to one side so they would be out of the pedestrians' way.

"There's no need for that," Victoria insisted with an offhand shrug. "Whenever I'm through with my shopping I'll make my own way home. I don't expect you to wait for me."

"But I might not make my way back." He tipped his dark head to one side. The prospect appeared to amuse him.

"This is an island. How could you get lost?" she laughed.

"I'm not taking any chances. Where shall I meet you?" Dirk persisted.

Victoria hesitated for an instant, then gave in. "Eleven-thirty at the Grand Hotel," she said and immediately started to walk away.

"Where is that?" he asked.

"You can't miss it. It boasts the longest front porch in the world," she called over her shoulder.

Before she looked to the front again, she saw his half salute of acknowledgement. Victoria didn't have much shopping to do. A stop at a drugstore made all her purchases—shampoo, polish remover, and cotton balls. She wandered along the sidewalk, looking in windows and entering a few places to say hello to shop owners she had known since childhood.

When eleven-thirty drew near Victoria found

her steps turning eagerly toward the Grand Hotel. She deliberately slowed them. She would be acting like Penny if she wasn't careful. But the silent admonition had no control over the way her heart somersaulted when she saw Dirk leaning against one of the pillars of the long white porch. She immediately looked away to pretend an interest in the bright yellow and red carpet of the flower beds. Her hand trailed along the yellow railing that lined the sidewalk on the opposite side of the street from the hotel. She crossed the street at the hotel's main entrance and climbed the steps to the famous porch. Dirk was there, having traversed the length of the porch to meet her.

"Did you get your shopping done?" His dark eyes glanced to the single package in her hand.

"Yes, I did," she nodded.

"Are your parents expecting us back for lunch?" Since his question didn't have a simple answer, Victoria hesitated and Dirk immediately guessed. "Obviously they aren't. So, why don't we have lunch before going back?"

Victoria was on the verge of refusing when she heard herself agreeing. "But only if we go dutch," she added.

"I wasn't going to buy your lunch. I was going to let you buy mine." The corners of his mouth were pulled down to form smiling grooves in his cheeks.

"Oh, you were?" Victoria laughed, not certain whether she should take him seriously.

"Yes, you can afford it more than I can," he replied.

"Oh, come now," she chided. "Your column is syndicated in practically every major newspaper in the country. You are very successful."

"Very successful, by most people's standards," Dirk qualified. "Let me put it this way. You probably spend more money on clothes than I do to live on during the period of a year. My bankbook couldn't match zeros with your father's."

"Is that your goal in life?" she challenged with faint criticism. "To make a lot of money?"

"I have a lot of ambitions. Not all of them have been realized yet. Naturally one of them is financial security, but it doesn't take as much money to satisfy me as it takes for you." His smile was aloof with the barest hint of contempt.

It roused Victoria's ire. "If you think I'm going to spend the rest of my time over lunch apologizing for the fact that I happened to be born into a wealthy family, then let's cancel it now," she informed him icily.

A flicker of genuine amusement entered his dark eyes. "Don't go all cool and highbred on me, Victoria. I thought we had progressed past that point," he murmured.

But she wasn't so easily soothed. "My parents were rich, and your parents were poor—" she began.

"And never the twain shall meet . . . except

over lunch." Dirk offered his arm to her, challenging her with his smile. "Shall we?" At Victoria's mutinous hesitation Dirk took her hand and slipped it on the inside of his left arm, spreading her fingers over his forearm with mocking formality. "I believe that's the way it's done," he taunted with insufferable arrogance and Victoria started to pull her hand free. His right hand closed around her fingers and pressed them to his arm with punishing strength. "You are sensitive, aren't you?" Both his voice and his look had a velvet quality that gently caressed and smoothed her ruffled fur.

"Considering the way you have been jabbing at me all day, is it so surprising?" Victoria defended.

"Have I?" His expression of disguised amusement heightened the sheer maleness of him and her heart thudded loudly against her ribs. "Over lunch, I promise no jabs . . . not even a tiny prick. Scout's honor." He raised his fingers in the Scout's pledge.

"Were you a Scout?" she doubted sharply.

"As a matter of fact," Dirk paused deliberately, a satanic light in his dark eyes, "no."

"That's what I thought," Victoria muttered.

A low chuckle came from his throat. "Come on." Without allowing her any more protests, Dirk escorted her inside the hotel to the restaurant.

When they were shown to a table heads turned, especially the female ones. Victoria could understand the effect Dirk had on a woman. After all, she knew he couldn't be trusted and here she was sitting down to eat with him anyway.

Dirk kept his word and their conversation over lunch was focused on impersonal topics. In spite of that Victoria found herself examining his every sentence for a double meaning. She tried to be pleasant, but could never manage to entirely lower her guard and be natural. Both of them refused dessert in favor of coffee.

Victoria sipped at hers, holding the cup in both her hands and swirling the coffee to cool it. "Where did you learn to speak French?" she asked. "In college?"

"No." Dirk set his cup down and peered at her through his lashes, amusement twitching his mouth. "About ten years ago, there was a French girl who lived in the same building as I did. She had only recently emigrated and knew very little English. I could understand when she was saying 'no,' but I wanted to be certain I knew when she was saying 'yes.' Between a French dictionary, a grammar book, and Jeanne, I learned French."

"Where is Jeanne now?" Victoria put her cup down because her hands suddenly felt a little shaky at the thought of saying 'yes' to him. She tried to sound nonchalant and undisturbed.

"I think she married a plumber." Dirk started to reach a hand into his shirt pocket, then paused. "Do you mind if I smoke?"

"No, go ahead," she insisted. "Were you in

love with her?'' she asked as she watched him light the cigarette.

"Do you want an honest answer to that?'' He slipped the butane lighter into his shirt pocket, his dark eyes bright with challenge.

"Yes.'' Victoria blinked, not understanding the reason for that question.

"Because I don't want to be accused of being crude,'' Dirk explained it. "No, I wasn't in love with her. I simply enjoyed going to bed with her.''

A flash fire of heat spread over her skin, but Victoria refused to let him see that his bluntness in any way disconcerted her, or that his remotely suggestive answer bothered her.

"Then you obviously learned when she said 'yes,' '' she murmured.

"Obviously,'' Dirk agreed dryly. His gaze narrowed slightly to glide over her face with smooth blackness. "With you it would be more difficult to decipher when you said 'yes.' I would have to surmount a class barrier instead of a language barrier.''

Victoria caught at the breath she was taking. "You seem determined to regard me as a snob.'' She let the breath escape in anger.

"And I promised not to prick, didn't I?'' he said with mock regret.

"I didn't really expect you to keep your word,'' she returned with icy calm.

"I was fantasizing again, trying to decide what it would take to persuade you to say 'yes,' ''

Dirk shrugged, his eyes not leaving her face, observing her every reaction.

"You have an overactive imagination," Victoria countered.

"I believe you've hinted at that before." His unconcern at the criticism appeared total.

"It deserves repeating."

"It's your fault."

"Mine?" Victoria repeated with wide-eyed indignation.

"Yes, either you shouldn't be so beautiful or else you shouldn't adopt that touch-me-not attitude. It challenges a man to poke it full of holes." There was an infuriating gleam in his eye and Victoria searched futilely for a suitably scathing retort.

"Victoria!" At the sound of her name, she turned to see a tall, statuesque woman of indeterminate age approaching the table. She recognized Daphne Bourns, a contemporary of her mother's. "It's been so long since I saw you last. Your mother stopped by last week to let us know you all had arrived on the island. How are you?"

"Fine, thank you, Mrs. Bourns."

The sophisticated brunette faked a wince. "Daphne," she corrected. "You make me sound as old as your mother." Which she was, although she looked closer to Dirk's age.

"You are so young at heart, Daphne, that sometimes you make me feel old," Victoria responded diplomatically.

"Flatterer," the woman laughed at the accusation and her brown eyes gazed pointedly at Victoria's companion. "Aren't you going to introduce me to this gorgeous hunk of man, Victoria? Or must I do it myself?"

With a sideways glance, Victoria saw that Dirk was standing in polite deference to the woman's presence. His expression was unfathomable in its regard of the still-very-attractive brunette.

"Of course. Daphne, this is Dirk Ramsey who is . . . visiting us." Victoria chose not to identify his profession. It was unlikely that Daphne knew his name since she rarely read anything but the society section of a newspaper. "This is Daphne Bourns, a friend of the family."

"It's a pleasure, Mrs. Bourns." Dirk acknowledged the introduction with a faint nod, the width of the table precluding a handshake.

"I'm sure the pleasure is distinctly mine," Daphne Bourns demurred. "Are you here getting acquainted with the family, Mr. Ramsey?"

"You could say that," he conceded with an amused twitch of his mouth.

The brunette turned to Victoria. "I had heard you had a guest. The island grapevine at work again," she explained her source in a laughing tone. "My, but you are a dark horse, Victoria. No one has even hinted that you had someone like this in the wings."

It was evident that Daphne had surmised Dirk was Victoria's boyfriend and his visit indicated the seriousness of their supposed romance. She probably suspected there was an engagement announcement in the offing.

"I think you misunderstood," Victoria inserted quickly. "Mr. Ramsey is a reporter, so this isn't strictly a social visit."

"Oh." Daphne's gaze ran a quick reassessment of Dirk. "I can't imagine it's all work and no play. You don't look a bit dull."

"I try to keep myself entertained," Dirk replied in a dry tone.

"How long will you be staying?" Daphne asked.

"I plan to be here two weeks." There was faint emphasis on the verb to indicate he might change his mind.

"Marvelous!" the brunette exclaimed in a husky voice. "You will be here for my party Saturday night. It's a formal little affair, my contribution to the lilac festivities." She directed her next sentence to Victoria. "Be sure to bring him, won't you, Victoria?"

"Of course," she smiled politely. If Daphne's party this year was typical of previous ones, Dirk's opinion of her and her family as high-class snobs would be reinforced. Their life-style on the island was usually very casual, but Daphne always insisted on throwing a very formal bash. Her reason was she wanted an excuse to dress up, and it probably was that simple.

"It's kind of you to include me," Dirk murmured.

The waitress paused at their table to leave the luncheon check. Dirk stopped her, glanced at the total, and placed the amount plus a tip on the metal tray before giving it back to the waitress.

"Kind?" Daphne repeated the word, a knowing gleam in her brown eyes. "I'm insuring my party is a success. An injection of new blood is just what our little group needs to liven it up a bit." With an infinitesimal shrug of her shoulders she gave them both a smile of reluctance. "I'm having lunch with some friends. I wish I had seen you earlier and you could have joined us. Perhaps you could have coffee with us?"

"Another time, perhaps," Victoria refused, trying to conceal the irritation gnawing at her poise. "We have to be going."

"Pity," she returned with a faint sigh. "I'll see you both Saturday, if not before. Take care."

"It was a pleasure meeting you, Mrs. Bourns," Dirk offered.

"Daphne." With a little wave of her hand she walked from the table.

"Divorced?" Dirk's hand was at the back of her chair to politely assist her when Victoria pushed from the table to give credence to her statement that they were leaving.

"No." She denied that Daphne was divorced. "She claims to be very happily married. Her daughter, however, is single." There was a faint bite to her voice, something malicious in its tone. It wasn't like her to be catty and Victoria didn't understand it.

"Is she like her mother?" His hand was at the back of her waist as Dirk guided her through the cluster of tables to the exit. His voice sounded only mildly interested.

"Shelly is more introverted," Victoria replied, again with the faint snap.

"I don't imagine that Mrs. Bourns is eager to share the spotlight," Dirk commented. They walked to the area in front of the hotel where they could obtain a horse-drawn taxi. "How old is her daughter? Your age?"

"No, she is—" Victoria had to think a second "—nineteen."

Daphne Bourns adored her daughter, but she also overshadowed her and wasn't aware of it. It was something Dirk had known instinctively. Inwardly Victoria had to agree with Dirk's observation that Daphne unconsciously competed with her daughter for attention, but it rankled that his guess had been so accurate on such short acquaintance.

After hiring a cab, Dirk helped her into the buggy seat and climbed in beside her. As the taxi pulled away from the curb Victoria opened her purse, counted out some money and offered it to Dirk.

Raising his eyebrows he gave her a sharply questioning look. "What's the purpose of that?"

"For my lunch." When he didn't take it she forced it into the palm of his hand.

"It isn't necessary." He held the bills between his middle and forefinger and offered them to her.

"I believe it is," Victoria insisted with a proud tilt to her chin as she stared straight ahead and ignored the money he held out to her. "The agreement was we would each pay our own."

"I didn't make any agreement if you recall," he replied lazily. "Buying your lunch won't break me."

"I'm sure it was an investment, one that is bound to pay you enormous dividends. Daphne was impressed when you picked up the check, but that was the purpose, wasn't it?" she challenged in dry sarcasm, tossing him a cool look.

"I beg your pardon." His voice was low and vibrant with controlled anger as his gaze narrowed to hard black points of light.

"Maybe you missed your calling," she suggested haughtily. "You would look very decorative on a woman's arm, more attention getting than furs or jewelry. Why, you could mingle with all the best people, vacation on the Riviera or at Acapulco. Every hostess would simply drool to have you accept an invitation to her party."

Dirk took her purse before Victoria could stop him and slipped the money inside. Snapping it closed he gave it back, his jaw clenched in hard anger.

"If I wanted to be a consort of the rich, I would be writing a society or gossip column instead of dealing with issues of corruption, energy, and crime." For all the glittering fire in his look, his voice was level and infuriatingly calm. "I fully intended to buy your lunch all along, and you will do me the courtesy of accepting."

It was impossible not to believe that he meant every word he had said. Victoria realized that she had wanted to think the worst, a discovery that didn't make her feel very proud.

"It appears that I might have been mistaken about your motives," she admitted with grudging reluctance.

"It does appear that way," Dirk repeated dryly and laid his arm along the back of the buggy seat.

For nearly a block neither of them spoke. The only sounds were the clip-clopping of the horse's hooves, the creaking of the buggy, and the whir of the wheels rolling over the road. A breeze stirred to life by their motion fanned the pale amber hair around her face. Victoria grew uncomfortable with the silence and half turned in her seat to face Dirk.

"You have to admit that your past behavior wouldn't exactly inspire me to trust you," Victoria justified. "Look at the way you attacked my father on the basis of circumstantial evidence without really ever knowing him."

"Circumstantial evidence can be very damning, but I admit the conclusions it suggests are not always accurate," Dirk conceded. "For example, when I look at you I see Italian shoes, a dress that probably boasts a London label—" after his gaze had lazily skimmed the expensive lavender material, he leaned slightly closer, "—and catch the fragrance of French perfume. On the surface you appear to be a walking advertisement for foreign goods, except . . . ." Dirk paused, a magically warm look entered his eyes that Victoria found dangerously fascinating. His hand shaped itself to the back of her neck, the contact freezing her into immobility. "Those lips are very American."

His firm grip prevented Victoria from drawing back from the steady approach of his mouth. As it came closer, her lashes automatically lowered. A breathless weakness fluttered through her at the easy possession of his kiss. Leisurely, his mouth explored the soft curves of her lips, demanding no more than her acquiescence. It was a heady investigation that teased her into wanting something more. But Dirk didn't give it as he moved away and untangled his fingers from the tawny silk of her hair. Victoria blinked once and looked away from his knowing regard.

She summoned the poise that was her defense. "And how do American lips compare with French?"

His mouth twitched at her cool question. "A little inexperienced but their passion is much more genuine."

"Naturally you would know." Victoria let a little of her irritation creep into the retort.

"Naturally." His voice was laced with droll amusement. "They call you Tory, don't they?"

"My parents do, and some of my closest friends," she admitted without inviting him to take the privilege. Her phrasing was deliberately designed to exclude him from that select group.

"I wonder if you are really a conservative," Dirk mused. "Or whether there might not be some latent liberal traits."

"I have always made it a rule never to discuss politics . . . especially with reporters, Mr. Ramsey," Victoria countered smoothly.

"Dirk," he corrected with an easy laugh. "You forgot to stab with the name. It's much more effective when you do."

Victoria despaired of ever finding a way to penetrate that complacent exterior of his. He always seemed so totally in command of every situation, and she always felt maneuvered. With a barely concealed sigh Victoria turned her head to view the scenery the buggy was passing.

"This is a beautiful island," Dirk remarked.

Again, Victoria was shaken by the impression he was diverting the conversation to a safer topic because he knew she couldn't cope with the sexual double-talk they had been exchanging. And it was true.

"It's a very historic place, too." Victoria accepted the new topic and elaborated on it. "There are many places to see."

"Yes, I noticed the old fort when we flew in."

"It's still in its original form. It was built by the British during the American Revolution and

used again by them during the War of 1812."
She was beginning to sound ridiculously like a
tour guide and immediately stopped talking.

"Can I persuade you to take me on a tour of
the island some day while I'm here?" He eyed
her with a wicked glint as if he had been reading
her mind.

"You would learn more if you took the of-
ficial State Park Carriage tour," Victoria
countered.

"Yes, but I might have a guide that would
resemble the horses. You are easier on the eye, if
a little disturbing to the senses," Dirk replied.

"I find it hard to believe anything would
disturb you." She had a little trouble breathing
normally after that provocative comment.

"You do." When she didn't respond, he gave
her a mocking look. "Isn't that what you
wanted to hear?"

"Not particularly." She shook her head, trying to rid herself of the sensual tension in the at-
mosphere.

The trees thinned out as the horse-drawn taxi
turned into the driveway that curved in front of
the two-story stucco and brick home trimmed in
dark wood. It seemed a short ride, but Victoria
was relieved it was almost over.

"Here is your package." Dirk handed her the
bag she had wedged between them on the seat, a
paper barrier that really hadn't protected her
very well from his unsettling presence.

"Thank you." She took it as the buggy stopped in front of the main entrance.

Dirk stepped out first to help her down. Remembering the last time Victoria kept her arms rigidly straight to maintain a distance. Her feet touched the ground a foot from where he was standing.

Dirk paid the driver and held up a silencing hand when she began a protest. "No arguments."

"Or else?" she challenged, ignoring the driver who was smiling at their exchange as he clicked to his horse.

"Or else I really will believe you are one of those spoiled, little rich girls who always wants her way," he replied.

A threat would have been preferable to that comment. Now she didn't dare argue, which had been his aim all along. Simmering behind the mask of composure Victoria walked to the sheltered roof of the entryway.

Before she reached the door, the iron gate to the breezeway and terrace swung open with a rasping protest of metal. Penny came gliding through, feigning surprise when she saw Dirk and Victoria.

"Hello, you made it back, I see," she smiled brightly and Victoria knew her sister wasn't addressing her.

"Safe and sound," Dirk agreed with a hint of a different kind of amusement in his smile.

"Dad wanted to see you, something about fishing, I think," Penny passed the message on to Dirk. Victoria decided that explained why her younger sister was dressed in the belled slacks and white top—and why the nautical hat was perched so saucily atop her blond head.

"Thanks." Dirk opened the front door and held it for Victoria.

"Oh, Tory, can I talk to you for a minute?" Penny asked with feigned nonchalance. Taking the affirmative answer for granted she turned and walked back through the open gates to the breezeway. Victoria followed.

"What is it you wanted, Penny?" She had a pretty good idea.

"I want to borrow your red Windbreaker."

"Going fishing?" Victoria couldn't help teasing just a little.

"Yes, dad asked me to go with them . . . him," she corrected, instantly on the defensive. Just as quickly Penny changed to attack. "Honestly, Tory, I don't know whatever possessed you to invite Dirk along with you this morning."

"I didn't invite him, he invited himself," Victoria made that point clear.

"Either way you shouldn't have stayed gone all morning," Penny retorted. "Someone should remind you that Dirk is here because he wants to talk with dad."

"I think I am more aware of the reason for his visit than you are." Victoria found her younger sister's criticism a little irritating.

"If you are, then you shouldn't be monopolizing Dirk's time. I realize you must be desperate for a man to pay some attention to you, but—'' Penny was giving a very good imitation of adult disdain.

''Listen, little girl,'' Victoria interrupted in seething anger. ''You had better hold your jealous little tongue until you know what you are talking about, because Dirk Ramsey is the last man that I would want any attention from. And before you make a complete and utter fool of yourself, you might remember that he is twice your age!''

She saw the tears spring into Penny's eyes and the veneer of adulthood shatter. Victoria immediately regretted that she had been so harsh and angry, but it was too late. Whirling away on a choked sob, Penny dashed into the house with her long hair trailing like a blond cloud behind her.

''He has us fighting among ourselves now,'' Victoria murmured and bit at her lower lip. ''Divide and conquer.''

CHAPTER SIX

EVERYONE WENT FISHING except Victoria. Her mother tried to persuade her to come with them, but Victoria was adamant in her refusal. Her reason was twofold. The tension of the morning with Dirk had not left her, and Penny would undoubtedly think she was competing for Dirk's attention. Josie sent the fishing party off with a basket of sandwiches, snacks, and cold drinks in case they were late returning.

It was late in the evening before they trouped into the kitchen with their catch. Victoria was there helping Josie with the night's meal so it would be ready within minutes of the fishing party's return. She looked up from the relish tray she was preparing when the boisterous group entered the kitchen. Her glance ricocheted off Dirk's lazily smiling countenance to encompass her parents and sister.

"Did you have a good time?" Victoria asked pleasantly, although their happy, flushed faces revealed the answer.

"The best!" Penny declared and sent a sideways glance at Dirk.

"Josie, I heard you wishing the other day for

some really fresh fish. Here you are!'' Charles Beaumont proudly deposited their catch in the sink. ''How is that?''

The housekeeper exclaimed over them as if she had discovered a treasure. Victoria looked in the sink at the fish and added her praise of their size to Josie's, then returned to the side counter to finish the relish tray. Dirk leaned a hip against the counter near where she was working. Victoria became conscious of how small the horseshoe-shaped kitchen suddenly seemed.

''Mmm, stuffed olives, my favorite,'' Dirk observed and reached to take a half dozen from the tray.

''Quit stealing.'' She started to tap at his hand with the side of the fork she held, but it was already out of striking distance.

''Stealing, am I?'' he challenged softly and forced an olive between her lips, his fingers lingering on the lower curve after her teeth had bitten into the olive. ''You're eating them, too, so that makes you equally guilty.''

''No, it doesn't,'' Victoria denied and wished he would move away. That plaid shirt and his snug-fitting denims gave him an earthy look that was vital and raw in its compulsion. A lake breeze had rumpled his raven hair and Victoria felt an urge to smooth it into place.

''You look very domestic.'' His intonation implied that looks were deceiving.

''I'm not lost in a kitchen,'' she retorted. She

stopped trying to field his remarks and began asking questions of her own. "How many fish did *you* catch?"

"Only two," Dirk answered and popped another olive into his mouth. "I'm not much of a fisherman." It didn't sound as though it bothered him.

Penny walked over in time to catch his reply. "You may not have caught the most, Dirk, but you caught the biggest." She came to his defense immediately.

"So I did." The warm look he gave Penny ignited a spark of anger in Victoria. He had no right to encourage Penny's infatuation.

Taking the nautical cap off her head, Penny raised on tiptoe to place it on top of Dirk's dark hair. "I crown you King of the Fishermen!" she declared all in fun.

"If I'm king, that entitles me to a kiss, doesn't it?" Dirk flirted with gentle mockery.

"Sure," Penny agreed, a shade breathlessly and Victoria wanted to scream.

But she was incapable of making even a strangled protest as Dirk bent and kissed Penny on her cheek very near the corner of her mouth. It looked innocent enough, but Victoria didn't like the expression in those mirror-black eyes. Instead of releasing Penny entirely, Dirk curved her to his side. Automatically her sister slid her arm behind his waist while he absently rubbed her shoulder. Victoria seethed at the way Penny was practically purring out loud.

She had to say something or burst. "Where

did a street boy like you learn to fish, Dirk?"
Victoria challenged with an undertone of sarcasm.

"I didn't, not as a boy," he replied. "In fact,
I was twenty-six before I ever had a fishing pole
in my hands. The owner of the weekly newspaper I worked for took me fishing one
weekend."

"What did you catch?" Penny tipped her
head back to look at him, her attitude
deliberately provocative.

"A few tree limbs and sunken logs—it took
me a while to get the knack of casting," Dirk
smiled. "Eventually I think I caught one fish,
but maybe not."

Victoria shot a glance at her parents. It appeared they didn't see anything wrong with Dirk
hugging their teenaged daughter. If she stayed
there another minute, Victoria knew she was going to knock Dirk's hand away and yank Penny
away from him, so she picked up the relish tray
and walked into the dining room. She dawdled
at the table, precisely arranging the place settings
of silverware.

"The table looks nice," her mother remarked
as she emerged from the kitchen. "I can always
tell when you set the table, Tory."

"Thank you. It's only fair that you should
derive some pleasure out of all that expensive
education you paid for me."

"Tory, I've never heard you sound so bitter."
Lena Beaumont frowned at her in surprise.

"I'm sorry, mom." Victoria ran her fingers

through the edges of her hair. "Pay no attention to me. Your *guest* has just made me touchy about certain things."

"Dirk?" Her mother sounded skeptical.

Had her mother defected to the enemy, too? Victoria wasn't in the mood to argue her case, so she simply shook her head and forced a smile to her mouth.

"I'm probably imagining everything." She shrugged. "Forget I said anything."

Her mother hesitated, then accepted the explanation. "Would you mind helping Josie in the kitchen for a few more minutes? I have to go wash this fish stuff off my hands and change."

"I don't mind," Victoria agreed even though it meant going back in the kitchen where Dirk was, and where she didn't want to be.

As her mother left Victoria walked to the kitchen door and collided with Dirk who was just coming out. His reaction was instantaneous, grabbing her shoulders when she bumped into him. The steadying grip of his hands only added to her confusion. When she lifted her gaze, Victoria saw Penny's cap still on top of his head and was immediately filled with a cold rage.

"Would the king let me by?" Her voice was chilling, but her gray eyes were blazing.

His gaze narrowed on her for a long second. "Being a king doesn't suit me. You wear the crown since you enjoy looking 'down' on people." As he released her he took the hat from his head and put it on hers, then walked around her and out of the room.

Victoria stared after him, her throat tight with some unknown emotion. Turning, she pushed open the kitchen door and walked through. The cap slipped and she whisked it off, tossing it to Penny.

"Take care of that," Victoria ordered. "And you'd better get cleaned up. Don't think you are going to sit at the dinner table smelling and looking like that, because you aren't."

Penny bristled at the barrage of tactless orders. "You don't have any right to tell me what to do, Victoria Beaumont! I'm not a child so don't try to order me around."

"Stop being so sensitive and go wash," she retorted in frowning irritation.

"I'll go when I'm ready," Penny answered defiantly. "You don't give the orders around here."

"No, I do," Josie interceded between the quarreling pair. "This is my kitchen and *I* am telling you to go. *Vite!*"

Penny didn't dispute Josie's authority, although she showed her displeasure by storming out of the room. Victoria's anger was revealed in the rigidity of her carriage.

"She needs a good shaking!" she declared and walked stiffly to the stove. She lifted lids on the pots without noticing the contents and let them clatter back into place. "Did you notice the way he put his arm around her? It was disgusting!"

"*Je* . . . ." Josie started to reply in French, then appeared to realize that Victoria's mood was not conducive to translation. "I think you might be wishing his arm had been around you."

"That's preposterous!" she denied absolutely.

"You should open your eyes, Victoria, before he decides to open them for you," the housekeeper warned.

"My eyes are open," Victoria assured her.

"Then why pretend that you weren't a little jealous of your sister?" Josie countered with a tiny smile edging the corners of her mouth.

"There isn't any point in discussing this with you. You don't understand," she declared in exasperation.

When she sat down to the table a quarter of an hour later, Victoria didn't have any appetite for the food she had helped prepare. She excused herself as soon as she decently could and went up to her room.

AFTER A NIGHT'S SLEEP and a slim breakfast, Victoria discovered that she felt just as unsettled and restless as she had the previous night. The obvious solution was to burn up the nervous energy that was making her on edge. She changed out of the slacks and blouse she had put on when she'd gotten up, and into a pair of brief white shorts and a blue knit top.

Downstairs, she exited the house through the sliding door to the breezeway and walked directly to the garage. Her bicycle was parked in front of the overhead door. Victoria flipped the switch that would raise it. There was a faint whir as the door lifted. When it was up Victoria walked to her bike.

"Good morning. I thought I heard the garage door opening and wondered if I was imagining things," Dirk said as he wandered into view. "Going somewhere?"

"I'm taking my bike out. I need some exercise," she explained shortly and took hold of the handlebars to wheel it outside.

"I'm beginning to feel a little sedentary, too. You wouldn't have another bike I could use? I'll ride with you."

"Only Penny's, and it has a flat tire," Victoria was glad to say. "Sorry."

"What's this?" Dirk spied something in the garage and went to investigate it. "It's a bicycle built for two. I've never ridden one of these things," he declared in a faintly bemused voice.

"It's mom and dad's. I don't think they've ridden it since last summer. It might be broken," Victoria hoped, then added maliciously. "Besides, where did you learn how to ride a bike? I thought you were poor as a child."

"But I had an old motorcycle when I was seventeen, because it gave me a cheap form of transportation." The glitter in his dark eyes laughed at her attempt to put him down. "It was a few years later before I tested my cycling skills on a bike. It's mostly a matter of balance and leg power." He pushed the kickstand back and guided the two-seater bike out of the garage. All the tires were inflated and nothing seemed to be wrong with the chains. "What do you say?"

Dirk glanced at her. "Are you game for a ride on this?"

There was a silent challenge in his question, but it was the eagerness in his look that Victoria responded to. He had never ridden a bicycle built for two and he wanted to find out what it was like.

"All right," she agreed, "as long as you promise not to start singing 'Daisy, Daisy, give me your answer true.' "

"You have my word," he chuckled, "even if you are taking some of the fun out of it. How about if I hum it?"

In spite of herself Victoria found she was laughing right along with him. "I don't care," she declared in a laughing breath and wheeled her bicycle back into the garage.

"Do you want the front seat or the rear?" Dirk asked.

"You take the front," she said and turned so he wouldn't see the impish light in her gray eyes.

At first the bike was unwieldy until they adjusted to the weight of a second person and balanced themselves accordingly. They were both laughing as they wobbled the first few feet, threatening to crash any second, but the coordination eventually came.

"No backseat driving is allowed," Dirk reminded her when they were safely under way.

"I wouldn't dream of it," Victoria assured him, that gleam still in her eyes.

She had already discovered that it wasn't wise to concentrate too much on the scenery they were riding past. When she did, she tended to try to turn the fake pair of handlebars, which invariably threw them off balance. It was better to spend most of her time looking straight ahead, which meant looking at the back of Dirk's head and the breadth of his shoulders. Victoria didn't really mind that. In fact, it was interesting to watch the play of the muscles in his shoulders and back beneath the thin cotton material of his shirt, and to notice the changing shades of his black hair in different light—the blue black of the raven in the sunshine and coal black in the shadows of the trees.

They hadn't gone far when the road began to make a gradual rise. It was a gentle slope, not at all steep. Carefully Victoria lifted her feet off the pedals and rested them on the crossbar, letting Dirk do all the work to get them up the small hill. Before they reached the top he was standing in the pedals.

"It didn't look this steep, did it?" he said to her, his breathing only slightly labored.

"No, it certainly didn't," Victoria agreed, hardly able to keep the laughter out of her voice.

Dirk must have caught a hint of it, because he looked back and saw she wasn't helping him pedal up the incline. By then they had reached the top and he sat down on the seat.

"No wonder." Shaking his head, he applied

the brakes and slowed the bike to a stop. "Thought you'd get a free ride, did you? And let me do all the work?" He half turned to look at her, an amused and mock-threatening smile on his face.

"I couldn't resist it," Victoria defended her action, trying hard to keep the laughter from bubbling through.

"You think it's funny, do you?" he challenged. "Maybe it is. I'll have to find out for myself." Dirk stepped away from the bike and it nearly slipped to the ground before Victoria could right it. "We're going to change places so you can chauffeur me for awhile."

"Come on. It was just a joke," she coaxed.

"I know, but it's my turn to laugh." After setting up the kickstand to support the bike, Dirk hooked an arm around her waist and lifted her up and over the crossbars of the bike. Her cries of protest were lost in the laughter she couldn't stop. In the end, she was set on the front seat and Dirk climbed onto the rear.

"I'll never make it." Victoria glanced over her shoulder in a last plea. She had laughed so hard that she could hardly breathe.

"Try," Dirk ordered.

From the top of the hill the road sloped down. All Victoria had to do the first few hundred feet was to let the bike coast. With their combined weights they soon picked up speed. When the road leveled out it wasn't long before Victoria had to rely on pedal power. Gamely she tried.

The bike slowed to a crawl and she finally had to stop to catch her breath.

"It isn't fair," she panted. "You are too heavy."

"What do you think you are? Thistledown?" he chuckled "You read too many romances." But his feet moved to his set of pedals to help when they did start out again.

"Do you want to change places or shall I do the steering?" Victoria asked after she had gotten back her wind.

"No, you can drive."

"My, but you are a trusting soul," she mocked.

"I don't know that I would trust you with my soul," Dirk replied in a dry, taunting voice. "You might get careless with it. But I will trust you to steer the bike."

Victoria put a foot on the pedal in preparation for starting out while the other foot remained on the ground for balance. She glanced over her shoulder to meet the steady and vaguely challenging regard of his dark gaze.

"Whatever happens, happens to me first, is that the theory?" she chided with an unmistakable sparkle of laughter in her gray eyes.

"You guessed it, honey." His mouth curved lazily into a half smile.

The casual endearment was offered indifferently, but her senses responded to it with anything but indifference, stimulated by the natural caressing timbre of his voice. Her pulse fluttered in her chest, briefly interfering with her breath, as Victoria faced the front again and pushed off to start pedaling.

During the continuing ride, Victoria had a greater awareness of the man behind her. This subtle disturbance was not altogether unpleasant. In fact it was vaguely exhilarating, something Victoria couldn't explain and tried to rationalize away as a result of the invigorating exercise.

The rocky ground offered a grass-tufted clearing to the right of the road. When Victoria saw it she pointed to it and suggested, "Shall we stop there for a breather?"

"Why not?"

At his offhand agreement, Victoria guided the bike to the edge of the road. When the front wheel bumped into the uneven ground she braked and stepped off to balance the bike's unwieldy length. With Dirk's help she wheeled it off the road and leaned it against a tree.

In the center of the clearing, a breeze was cooling the sun-warmed air. Slightly warmed herself by the exertion and the morning sun, Victoria moved toward the center and lifted the hair away from her neck to let the fingers of the breeze cool her skin.

"Just a minute." Dirk's voice made her pause. "You have a thread hanging."

"Where?" Victoria stopped and tried to twist around to look behind her, a virtually impossible task.

"I'll get it," he volunteered and started to crouch behind her.

Victoria couldn't see the thread, but she could feel it dangling from the hem of her shorts, just barely brushing the back of her thigh. The discovery of its location coming right on the heels of his offer flamed her skin.

"No, I'll do it," she hurried the protest and tried to turn away.

"You can't even see it," Dirk chided while his hand clasped her hip to prevent her from moving out of his reach. "Stand still."

Struggling would only turn a slightly embarrassing situation into a humiliating one, so Victoria rigidly obeyed his command rather than display an exaggerated modesty. It wasn't easy to stand motionless under the firm touch of his hands. They seemed to burn through the brevity of her shorts as Dirk twisted the thread around his forefinger, a knuckle digging into the bare flesh of her thigh. On the surface his action was impersonal, but underneath there was an implied intimacy dictated by the very location of the problem. With a quick tug his hand pressed against her rounded flesh and the thread snapped. A riptide of heat coursed over her flesh.

"There you are." Dirk straightened and held out the white thread for her inspection.

Victoria couldn't meet his smiling glance. "Thank you." The words were as stiff as her posture.

When she took an escaping step forward, his

hand settled on her waist while he kept pace. Her rigidity was transmitted immediately to him. Dirk tipped his head to one side in an inquiring angle, his dark eyes running over her profile.

"What's the matter?" He sounded faintly bemused and curious.

"Nothing," she insisted.

By lengthening his stride, Dirk moved a half a step ahead of her and stopped to block her way. When she tried to go around him, his hand moved to capture her chin and lift it so he could see the expression she was trying to avoid showing him.

"I believe you are embarrassed." A wondering amusement laced his accusation and Victoria couldn't lift her gaze beyond the tanned column of his neck. She was fully aware of the hot stain that flushed her cheeks. Her discomfort wasn't improved by his closeness. "There is no need to be." His hand glided from the curve of her waist to the rounded flesh of her buttock, lessening the distance between them to inches. The ease of his familiar caress trembled through Victoria although she tried desperately not to show he was creating any disturbance. "I'm already familiar with every curve and muscle back there," Dirk murmured. "I've been watching it on that bike for long enough."

The breath Victoria tried to take never got farther than her throat, lodging there at his provocative comment. Her gaze rushed up to become trapped in the enveloping blackness of his. At the catapulting leap of her pulse, a flurry of sensations left her defenseless. When his mouth opened possessively on her lips, Victoria was launched into a heady plane where only man and woman existed. She responded hungrily to his devouring kiss, feeding his desire and being fed.

His hand moved in a long, leisurely caress from her chin, down her throat, across her shoulder, and around her back. Its sensual persuasion brought her fully against his length, her soft curves imprinted by the hard, male contours of his shape from the muscled wall of his chest flattening her breasts to the oak-solid trunks of his legs scraping the bareness of hers.

The drugging mastery of his kiss was narcotic and Victoria felt its addictive prowess asserting its hold on her. Under the languid domination of his mouth, she was dazzled by the slow-burning flames that grew ever more consuming. Her arms had encircled him. Her hands were reveling in the feel of the flexing and distending muscles in his shoulders and back.

An inner voice was trying to remind her of something unpleasant. Victoria knew if she listened to it, it would spoil the delicious joy she was experiencing. So she ignored the unintelligible warning in favor of the dangerous pleasure of the moment.

Disappointment raged when Dirk's hunger for her lips became satiated and his mouth was slowly removed from hers. Pride lowered her face to hide the fiery needs his kiss had kindled. Trembling with a blissful weakness, Victoria had to cling to him for support. Beneath her cheek, she could hear the hard thud of his heart and derived some measure of satisfaction from its loud beat.

His warm breath stirred the hair on her forehead and she inhaled his intoxicating, earthy smell. When his hand cupped the side of her face, Victoria didn't resist the pressure it exerted to lift her head. Those few minutes had given her time to conceal the wild disturbance his embrace had caused. Now Victoria found herself needing the reason why Dirk had initiated it.

The simplest and possibly the quickest solution was simply to ask. "Why did you kiss me?"

While his hand slowly caressed her cheek and jaw and the little hollow below her ear, his thumb lazily traced the outline of her lips, feeling the warmth and moistness that remained from his kiss.

"For a multitude of reasons," Dirk replied with a husky pitch to his voice. "The most obvious one is that you are a beautiful woman. I wanted to feel the softness of your body and mouth against my own."

Victoria needed something more complicated than that. It was too close to her own very basic reaction; therefore, the elemental attraction became too dangerous a premise to accept. Besides, his exploring thumb had parted her lips to probe at the white barrier of her teeth, its investigation too blatantly sensuous. Withdrawing her arms from around him, Victoria reached up to pull his hand from her face, and the thumb from lips that tasted the rough, salty texture of its skin.

"Your other reasons?" she prompted as the male hand she had been holding reversed the possession to hold her hand within its grip.

His mouth quirked briefly before he bent his head to press her fingertips against his lips and peer at her through the thick, male screen of his lashes. "To discover what I already suspected. There is a strong streak of liberalism in you, Tory. That cool composure of yours is only a mask worn by a warm, vibrant woman to hide the rawly passionate side that she hasn't learned to deal with yet." There was something very seductive in his veiled, but steady regard.

Her heart began beating at triple speed, instinctively knowing that Dirk could expertly teach her how to deal with her passions. With a fluttering of panic, Victoria freed her hand from his evocative nibblings and stepped away. Folding her arms in front of her nervously churning stomach she walked to the center of the clearing. Apprehensively, she sneaked a backward glance at Dirk to see if he was pursuing. He had moved generally in her direction, but he had stopped on a stretch of grass-carpeted earth to lower his muscled frame to the ground. Victoria felt a twinge of regret and hated herself for it.

"There's plenty of room." Dirk indicated the wide patch of grass to his left. "Why don't you join me?"

CHAPTER SEVEN

VICTORIA WAS TEMPTED, but the knowing glint in his eyes revealed that he expected an affirmative response. "No." With a quick shake of her head, she refused. The length of rough green earth reminded her too much of a blanket on the ground. Dirk continued to watch her, waiting for an explanation. She didn't want to admit it was his nearness combined with a horizontal position that bothered her, so she chose a much more mundane excuse. "I don't want grass stains on my white shorts. They might not come out."

"Is that all that's stopping you?" But Dirk said it as a statement despite its question form.

His reply puzzled her, but not nearly as much as his following action when he began unbuttoning his shirt and tugging it free from the waistband of his slacks. Her gray eyes widened as his bronze torso began to be revealed.

"What are you doing?" The faint tremor in her demand exposed her own susceptibility to the sight of so much masculine flesh, and the feathery cloud of raven chest hair.

Dirk shrugged out of the shirt, muscles rippling in the sunlight, and spread it on the ground beside him. "You can sit on my shirt and you won't have to worry about grass stains."

"B-but . . . ." Victoria searched helplessly for another reason, stunned by his action, while trying to maintain her poise.

"Isn't that chivalrous enough for you, little princess?" he mocked. "Wouldn't a true gallant spread his coat over a mud puddle? I don't have a coat, and there isn't any mud puddle. So the shirt and grass will have to do."

"Your shirt will end up with grass stains." She sought in vain for a convincing excuse to refuse.

"My shirt is considerably less expensive than those designer shorts you are wearing. Besides, a highborn lady like yourself shouldn't be concerned with a lowly servant's clothes." He was deliberately taunting her.

Victoria guessed that Dirk expected her to refuse his shirt and sit on the grass beside him to prove she wasn't a spoiled snob. She intended to show him that she wasn't so easily maneuvered. Her mouth curved into a smile, but there was a hard glitter in her gray eyes.

"You are quite right," she declared. "Why should I worry about your shirt?" She walked over and sat down squarely in the middle of it, wiggling a little to rub the cotton material into the grass and guarantee a stain.

"You little brat." Instead of being angry, Dirk chuckled with open amusement at her audacity.

"You said it," Victoria reminded him. "Better your shirt than my shorts." She leaned back on her hands, challenging him with a look.

"You don't think you are going to get away with it, do you?" Dirk turned to face her. Suddenly the distance between them wasn't nearly as much as it had seemed as a wall of bronze flesh loomed beside her.

Victoria regretted the desire for retaliation that had brought her to this half-horizontal position. An uneasiness sifted through her bones, followed immediately by a quivering awareness of how it had been to be in his arms.

"I'm sorry about your shirt," she apologized. "You made me angry when you said those ridiculous things about me. I really don't care about sitting on your shirt."

She would have moved to pull it out from beneath her, but his hand spread itself on the bare flesh of her thigh, on the opposite leg from where he was reclining.

"No, you don't," Dirk warned. "The damage is already done. Now you are going to sit there."

"It's your fault," Victoria defended in a voice that wasn't as steady as she wanted it to sound.

"No, it's your fault," he countered and leaned toward her, "for teasing me with one kiss and walking away."

"I wasn't teasing." With the hand on her thigh she couldn't scoot away, so Victoria attempted to escape his continuing approach by leaning farther and farther backward.

"I'm relieved to hear you weren't teasing."
His dark eyes mocked her as he followed her
down.

When his mouth was inches from hers, tan-
talizing her with its silent male promise, Victoria
whispered, "I don't want this to happen."

"Liar," Dirk murmured and let his mouth do
the rest of the convincing.

Under its pervading skill she tried to summon
a resistance, but his mouth claimed hers with a
sensual, leisurely thoroughness. Its intoxicating
potency sent a tremor of weakness through her
limbs. Fingers that had wound into the blades of
grass released the green tufts to hesitantly seek
the warm male skin stretched so firmly across
the muscled expanse of his shoulders and back.
He penetrated her lips to languidly possess the
inner reaches of her mouth and rekindle the hot
fires that had consumed her only moments
before.

The crushing weight of him was eased to one
side as he forced an arm under her to mold her
to his will. Victoria shifted to more easily accom-
modate his arm and enjoy the searing fire of his
kiss. His free hand had left her hip and was exploring her waist. Having enslaved her lips, Dirk
left it to wander to her throat, nibbling at the
highly sensitive skin at the hollow.

Her breath was little more than sighing gasps
of reluctant pleasure. Victoria bit her lip to try
to keep it from escaping to betray her any more
than her flesh and her senses were already doing.

When his fingers slipped under the cotton of her T-shirt, her hand slid along his hair-roughened arm in an effort to stop this suddenly intimate exploration of his hand. Her effort was puny at best, and the skin covering her rib cage quivered in traitorous excitement at the caressing touch of his hand.

As if sensing this inner resistance, Dirk's mouth returned to her lips to quell this minor revolt before it gained strength. When he found her teeth in possession of her lower lip, he let his tongue trace the outline, teasing until her mouth was turning to find his. While her senses had been occupied with the tormenting nearness of his mouth, his hand had moved upward to cup her breast and stir the peak into hardness beneath the silken material of her brassiere. A sweet, consuming ache began in her midsection and spread lower. Victoria stiffened at its cause.

"Let go." His mouth laid a molten trail over her face, his caress as seductive as his voice. "Let go, Tory, and let that wonderful aching confusion become rapture."

The temptation to yield to his promise was potent, but Victoria twisted her head far to the side. "No," she choked out the denial and continued in a hoarse anger. "I am sure it would make quite an exclusive story to have bedded Charles Beaumont's daughter, but you aren't going to get it."

When he lifted his head to glare at her in surprise, Victoria took advantage of his action to roll from beneath him and onto her feet.

"Do you believe what you just said?" Dirk demanded, rising to stand behind her.

"Do you deny that it's true?" she retorted without looking at him.

"It would probably make a hell of a story, but I don't write for the scandal sheets!" he snapped and bent to whip his shirt from the ground. "As a matter of fact, I had forgotten you were even related to Charles Beaumont!"

Turning, Victoria watched him buttoning his shirt. She couldn't tell by his expression whether that barely contained anger had been genuine or faked. Dirk glanced up and caught her narrowed and wary look. Tucking his shirt into his pants, he walked over to her.

"You don't seem to have much confidence in yourself as a woman. Why, Tory?" His dark gaze pinned her.

"Don't call me that." She avoided his question. "It's a name reserved for my family and very close friends."

"And what am I?" His gaze raked her to remind her of how close they had been. "Or is it my background that precludes me from that select group? Maybe I should call you *Miss* Victoria?" His strong white teeth were biting out the words.

"No!" Victoria angrily denied that she wanted that. "And it isn't your background! It's your profession." She cooled her voice to a more normal level. "I don't trust you, and you have given me very little cause to trust you."

His mouth quirked, grooves slashing deeply at

the corner. "Considering the way you affect my blood pressure, I would advise you not to trust me if I was wearing the robe of a celibate monk's order."

"Should I thank you for that?" Victoria resorted to sharpness, having no other defense against him. His provocative candor undermined the wariness she tried so hard to nurture.

"No, I don't want you to thank me for it," he mocked. "I want you to remember it." His hand reached out to snare the back of her neck and hold it still while his mouth bruised her lips in a hard, searing kiss. It ended with the same abruptness as its conception, but his face moved only inches from hers, his dark gaze burrowing deep into the confused gray of her eyes. "I'm told exercise is a more satisfactory release for sexual frustration than verbalizing. Shall we start for the house?" Not waiting for a reply, Dirk turned but didn't release his grip on her neck as he guided her to the tree where they had left the bicycle. "Only this time I'll take the front seat." His hand gently kneaded the back of her neck where his fingers had dug so punishingly into the flesh moments ago. "I think I have a better idea where we're going than you do."

Victoria opened her mouth to protest that statement, but Dirk had already turned away. No longer able to see the enigmatic glint in his eye, she couldn't be sure his comment had been as ambiguous as she had interpreted it.

"Are you ready?" When he glanced over his shoulder his look was bland and unreadable.

Was she imagining the double meaning? Victoria shook away the mental confusion and walked to the rear of the bike.

As she swung a leg over the crossbars, Dirk half turned to ask, "Is something bothering you?"

"You," she answered shortly without lifting her gaze from the handlebars.

"That's a start," he murmured and pushed the bike forward to walk it to the road.

There was no conversation during the long ride back, yet Dirk dominated her thoughts. A few short days ago she had actively disliked him. If asked whether she regarded him as an enemy her answer would have been an unequivocal yes. Now, when he had almost breached her defenses, Victoria found that she didn't resent him for it. There was a part of her that was sorry he failed.

The smear of yellowy green grass stain on the back of his shirt taunted Victoria. The thin cotton material hid the taut flesh her hands had so eagerly caressed, and longed to do again. Dirk wasn't the enemy. The enemy was within. Victoria didn't have to be on guard with him, but on guard against her own wayward inclinations.

At the garage Victoria got off the bike as soon as Dirk braked it to a stop. Eager to escape his unnerving company she was in a hurry to put the bike away, but Dirk took his time wheeling it into the garage.

"It's unsettling, isn't it?" He tossed out the curious remark with deceptive casualness.

"What is?" In spite of a little voice insisting that she didn't want to know the answer, Victoria asked the anticipated question.

"To . . . like someone that you were determined to dislike." Dirk hesitated deliberately over the word to imply the attraction was stronger than the word indicated.

"I really wouldn't know," she lied and hurriedly left the garage to let him maneuver the unwieldy bike into its rightful place.

In the breezeway she was confronted by her younger sister. Jealousy was behind the disdainful look Penny gave her, and only Victoria knew how much cause her little sister had to be jealous.

"A bicycle built for two? Really, Tory, how juvenile can you get?" Penny declared contemptuously.

"Don't look at me." Victoria attempted a cool defense. "It was Dirk's idea, not mine."

Surprise mixed with chagrin in her sister's expression. Victoria took advantage of the speechless moment to slip inside the house and upstairs to her room.

SHIFTING THE TENNIS RACKET to her other hand, Victoria pushed open the front door and walked inside. It had been unusually hot and sticky on the tennis court that afternoon. Foremost on her mind was a desire for a cold drink and cool shower.

Her rubber-soled shoes barely made any sound as she crossed the foyer, ignoring the stairs in favor of the vestibule and its door to the kitchen area. Pausing at the door Victoria was struck by the silence of the house, so strangely quiet. Even the kitchen was empty when she entered it. She looked curiously around, then walked to the refrigerator to take out the pitcher of lemonade. As she filled a tall glass from the cupboard, out of the corner of her eye she saw the housekeeper entering the kitchen.

"Hello, Josie."

"*Mon Dieu!*" The woman nearly dropped the bundle of neatly folded towels stacked in her arms.

"Did you think I was a ghost?" Victoria laughed and took a refreshing sip of the lemonade. "Where is everybody?"

The housekeeper was obviously suffering from shock since she lapsed into English to answer curtly, "I have more important things to do than keep track of the comings and goings of this family."

"Sorry I asked," Victoria murmured with an exaggerated lift of an eyebrow. "It's so late that usually everyone is home by now."

The comment drew the housekeeper's sharp glance at the wall clock. By her dismayed expression Victoria guessed that Josie hadn't realized what time it was. There was a sudden haste to her footsteps as she crossed the kitchen and unceremoniously forced the folded bath towels into Victoria's arms.

"I have to begin dinner," she explained. "Take these towels to M'sieur Ramsey's room."

Victoria hesitated, but it was a reasonable request since she was on her way upstairs to shower and change. She took another swallow of the lemonade before setting the glass down to arrange the towels in their previously neat order.

"I'll come back for my tennis racket," Victoria promised and received a grunting acknowledgement.

Leaving the kitchen through the door to the vestibule, she climbed the stairs to the second floor. As she neared the top, Victoria heard the tap-tap-tapping of a typewriter coming from Dirk's room. She paused at the head of the stairs. Her family might be gone, but Dirk obviously wasn't. Nibbling at her lower lip she wavered, then crossed the upper foyer to knock on his door. The towels were held in front of her like a shield.

The typing stopped; so did her heart. The scrape of a chair leg was followed by footsteps crossing the room to the door. She mentally braced herself and fixed a composed expression on her face as the door was opened. The preoccupied light left his dark eyes the instant he saw her. His gaze took on a velvet quality, stroking her as he surveyed her length and the bareness of her legs beneath the short white tennis skirt.

"I would have sworn you were the type who would bolt at the sight of a man's bedroom," he taunted.

"Josie asked me to bring you some clean towels," Victoria smoothly explained the reason for her presence.

She would have preferred to hand him the towels, but he stepped out of the doorway so she could enter. His arm made a casual sweep in the direction of the private bath.

"Hotels never seem to hire chambermaids who look like you," Dirk remarked. "Nor do their uniforms resemble yours."

"Probably with good reason." As she walked briskly past him toward the door to the private bath, her gaze was drawn to the typewriter on the narrow desk and the paper sticking out of its carriage. There was an intense curiosity to know what he was writing. Another article about her father, perhaps?

Dirk followed her as far as the door to the bathroom and leaned against the frame. "I take it you've been playing tennis."

"Yes, with some friends." Victoria arranged two sets of the towels on the brass racks and knelt to store the rest in the cupboard of the glazed tile lavatory.

"We still haven't played that tie breaker with your parents, have we?" he remembered. "We should set that up for tomorrow."

"I can't. I have other plans." She didn't know what those other plans were, but she would think of something. Straightening, she walked toward the doorway, arching an eyebrow in a silently arrogant request for Dirk to move.

With a faintly mocking nod of his head, he made a ninety-degree pivot to allow her past. "I have noticed that you have arranged to be busy these last couple of days," Dirk admitted with a knowing glint. "I guess I could ask your sister to partner me in a match with your parents."

"I'm sure she'd like that!" Victoria snapped, then halted to glare at him. "Why don't you leave the poor girl alone? You are old enough to be her father."

He feigned a wince. "An older brother, surely."

"Penny happens to be only sixteen," Victoria informed him.

"That young?" he mocked. "Then it is definitely a brotherly affection I have for her."

"Brotherly, ha!" There was a wretched tightness in her throat. "I doubt that you have ever regarded any female in a brotherly fashion."

Dirk eyed her with a lazily narrowed look. "Do you know you almost sound jealous, Tory?"

"That's absurd!" she denied. "Personally, I couldn't care less how much attention you pay to her. My only concern is the effect it's having on Penny."

"Of course," he murmured dryly in a tone of outright skepticism.

In agitation, Victoria turned away and took two steps. It was purely by accident that she had happened to move in the direction of the typewriter. The white paper with its typed words beckoned for her attention.

"I see you haven't been spending all your time corrupting my sister," she remarked and moved closer so she could read the words. "You have obviously managed to do some writing, too."

Before her hand could reach out to straighten the sheet of paper so she could read it, Dirk was there to cover it with the thick volume of a dictionary.

"Sorry." But the unyielding blackness of his eyes said he wasn't.

"You act as if you have something to hide," Victoria accused and reached to move the book. "What are you writing?"

His fingers closed around her wrist to stop her. "I don't let anybody read any of my material until I'm finished."

"Are you one of those temperamental creators?" she mocked and strained to twist her wrist free of his talonlike hold without success.

"Could be." Dirk shrugged noncommittally.

"What's the subject?" Victoria challenged, certain that it had to do with her father.

"Maybe my imagination is running rampant again," he suggested with a wicked glint.

"I wouldn't be at all surprised," she retorted.

"What do you suppose happens when two people who have always got what they wanted, are unexpectedly thrown together?" he mused, exerting just enough pressure on her arm to force her a few inches closer.

"I really wouldn't know." She heard the breathless catch in her voice, but couldn't do anything about it.

"Two people like us," Dirk continued. His free hand curved around her waist to enclose her inside the circle of his arm, indifferent to her attempt to keep a small space wedged between them with her arms on his chest. "You, who have always been given what you wanted, and me, who's always had to fight for what he wanted."

"I don't see the point," she protested.

"Don't you?" He released her wrist to let both of his arms gather her in, trapping her hands between them. "The solution would be to join sides, so we could both want the same thing."

He held her fast. To be in the sensuous clasp of his arms was like being in a velvet-lined straightjacket. The lower half of her body was firmly shaped to his length, her hips fitted into the cradle of his. Victoria felt the succumbing weakness spreading through her limbs.

"Will you please let me go?" Her voice was low and trembling in its demand.

"No, I don't think so." Dirk smiled and lowered his head.

She turned her head away, but he was satisfied to let his mouth trail over the curve of her neck, pausing to nibble sensually at an earlobe along the way. Shivers of pure delight danced over her skin to send tremors through her system. Dirk was in no hurry to find her mouth, letting his lips tease and tantalize every inch of her neck, ear, and cheek. All the while his caressing hands were roaming her back and hips, stirring raw needs and confusing her thoughts.

"Kiss me." His husky order came when Victoria's resistance was at its lowest ebb.

The sensual firmness of his mouth was only inches from her own. With masterful ease he had tuned her senses to his desire. Her lips parted even before they felt the warm contact of his. While she strained to respond to the demanding ardor of his kiss her hands glided around his neck to thread her fingers through the virile thickness of his black hair.

Dizzying waves of rapture rocked her until Victoria had to lean heavily against him for balance. The scorching fires ignited by his hard kiss swept through her bloodstream to curl her toes and melt her shape to his unyielding form. Dirk shifted her slightly in his arms, the driving force of his mouth tilting her head back onto the curve of his shoulder. His hands had slipped beneath the knit tank top of her tennis outfit and were exploring the pliant softness of her flesh. The ever-growing intimacy of his caress plummeted peaks and valleys and circled rosy crests until Victoria was driven to the edge of her endurance by the wild yearnings assaulting her. Through it all, a slender thread of sanity weaved into her consciousness.

"Dirk, stop," she breathed against his mouth, feeling the heat of his breath mingling with hers.

"Why?" He took a fraction of a second to answer as he let his mouth move over her lips, tracing their outline with his.

This half kiss was devastating to her train of thought. It was several seconds before Victoria could come up with a reason. "It's late. Josie is fixing dinner."

"I have the only thing I'm hungry for right here." His teeth made tiny love bites on her lower lip. Her own appetite wanted the same fulfillment as his.

Victoria tried once more. "I have to shower yet . . . and change," she whispered the weak excuse.

"We'll shower together. You wash me and I'll wash you." His hand slid from her rib cage to the center of her spine as he crushed her to his chest with a stifled groan and covered her mouth in a searing kiss.

CHAPTER EIGHT

IN THE FOYER the front door slammed. Someone came rushing up the stairs, taking the steps two at a time. Locked in a pair of arms she never wanted to leave, Victoria was only half-aware of the sounds intruding on the raw bliss of the moment.

"Dirk!" Penny's voice stabbed through the golden haze with a glaring white light. "I don't hear the typewriter." Her voice and half-running footsteps approached the guest room. "Have you finished the . . . ." Her voice stopped in midsentence as her footsteps halted at the open door.

Until that second Victoria had forgotten Dirk's bedroom door wasn't closed. Tearing her lips from the heady possession of his, her widened eyes sought the stricken face of the young girl in the doorway. The pain of disbelief and betrayal was in the suddenly brimming eyes of her sister. As if indifferent to the intruder Dirk continued to nuzzle Victoria's cheek. His arms were locked even tighter around her to prevent her from straining free of his embrace.

"Did you want something . . . Laurel?" Dirk asked without ever glancing at the doorway.

"How could you?" Penny accused on a choked sob. "She's so stuck-up and prissy, ..." There would have been more, but she couldn't hold back the tears. With a muffled cry she turned and fled to her room.

"Penny!" Victoria called after her and struggled to get loose. "You heard her coming," she accused Dirk. "Why didn't you remember the door was open? Why did you let her see us like this? That was cruel."

Dirk continued to hold her in the iron hook of one arm while his other hand captured her face and held it still. His knowing eyes examined her flushed face and lips swollen and soft from his kisses.

"It wouldn't have made any difference. She would have taken one look at you and guessed that I had been making love to you."

"But she didn't have to see," Victoria protested.

"Yes, she did," he insisted, "because she saw it was what I wanted. I don't want her having any delusions about which one of Charles Beaumont's daughters I'm interested in."

"You could have been more subtle," she accused.

"I could have," Dirk conceded with a careless shrug. "but this was swifter and more effective."

"You're a brute," she declared angrily. "Let me go. I have to talk to her and try to make her understand."

"Now?" he sighed reluctantly and let his gaze linger on her mouth.

"Yes, now!" Victoria wouldn't be sidetracked by more of his lovemaking and strained against his hold.

His arm loosened to let her go and Victoria didn't give him a chance to change his mind as she hurried out of the room into the second-floor foyer. At her sister's bedroom door she stopped. From inside the room she could hear Penny weeping uncontrollably. She tried the door, but it was locked.

Glancing over her shoulder she saw Dirk leaning against the framework of his door watching her. It was a certainty that Penny was no longer infatuated with him, Victoria was sure of that, but she considered his tactic to be callous. Considering who he was, she should have expected it.

With an abrupt pivot she walked to her bedroom. She and Penny shared an adjoining bathroom. Since those doors could only be locked from inside the bathroom, it was unlikely that her younger sister had even given them a thought. She hurried to the door and the knob turned easily in her hand. Her sister's muffled cries grew louder as Victoria crossed the fluffy carpet to the other connecting door.

When she opened it she saw Penny sprawled across the bed on her stomach, her face buried in the neck of a stuffed elephant. Her waist-length blond hair was fanned across her shoulders and arms, trembling like a golden silk curtain in a strong breeze as the young body heaved in wracking sobs. Penny was at such a sensitive age when feelings could be hurt so easily. Only this time they had been stomped on. Victoria moved toward the bed, her heart wringing in sympathy . . . and guilt because of the unwitting part she had played.

"Penny, I'm sorry," she murmured.

A blotched, tear-drenched face was lifted from the furry hide of the stuffed toy. "Go away!" Penny pushed the long strands of hair from the corner of her mouth, choking on the sobs that wouldn't stop. "I don't want you here!"

"I didn't mean to hurt you, Penny." Victoria knew the words were inadequate, but she wanted to comfort her young sister somehow. "It's the last thing I would do intentionally."

"You don't care!" Penny accused. "Neither do I because I hate you! I hate you!" Those words hurt, even though they were issued in the heat of unbearable pain. Unable to stop the tears Penny hid her face again in the toy elephant.

"Penny—" Victoria tried again.

"Go away!" Penny hurled the elephant in her direction, then wrapped her arms around a stuffed giraffe, part of her menagerie of toy animals that adorned the room, and hugged it tightly, shielding her face behind its slim neck.

Her aim was poor and the elephant missed Victoria by a foot. It was a second before she realized that she hadn't heard it hit the floor behind her. She turned and Dirk was standing inside the room, holding the stuffed animal he'd caught.

"What are you doing here?" she hissed under her breath. "Penny doesn't want to see you."

"I am exactly the person she wants to see," he corrected. "It's my apology she wants, not yours." He stepped out of the doorway to the bathroom so Victoria could leave.

"I'm staying," she insisted, continuing to speak in the low undertone as he had done.

Tossing the elephant in the corner, Dirk caught at her hand and pulled her toward the door. When she was level with him, he took hold of her shoulders and pushed her toward the bathroom.

"No, you aren't. Penny and I are going to talk this out in private," he stated. "Since we aren't going to be able to have that shower together, you might as well take yours now and get cleaned up for dinner."

He gave her a little shove into the bathroom and turned to the girl on the bed whose sobs had drowned out their muted conversation. But Victoria didn't immediately follow his orders. Instead, she stood in the bathroom and watched as Dirk walked to the bed and sat on the edge of it. His hand reached out to stroke the back of Penny's head.

"Hey, golden girl," he murmured softly.

Penny's muffled reply was a hurt, "How could you?"

"Broken hearts hurt, don't they?" Dirk

smiled as he gently turned the sobbing girl on her side.

Victoria watched Penny look up at him. Her sister's chin quivered, then her arms were reaching out for him and Dirk gathered her into the comforting circle. The stuffed animals were forsaken in favor of crying on the hard pillow of his chest. Strangely it didn't make Victoria feel better that Dirk was the one who was able to comfort her sister when her efforts had failed. She closed the bathroom door to Penny's room and locked it.

In her bedroom, she mulled over her confusing reaction. It wasn't jealousy. Was it envy? Did she wish that Dirk would be that gentle with her, comforting her, instead of turning her world topsy-turvy with his kisses? Laying out a pair of white slacks and a slate gray velour top, Victoria took her robe and entered the bathroom.

There were only muted sounds from Penny's room, indistinguishable. They were soon drowned out by the water rushing from the shower spray. It wasn't the most relaxing shower Victoria had ever taken. Every time she closed her eyes she kept imagining Dirk standing beneath the jets of water with her. The pelting spray reminded her flesh of how it had tingled under his carressing hands, awakening yearnings that until now had been easily controlled.

Her stomach was tied in knots when she stepped out of the shower. With the faucets turned off there was a murmur of voices from the adjoining bedroom, both Dirk's and Penny's. She heard Penny blow her nose, which obviously meant the crying was over. Victoria found such irony in the situation. A touch, a soft word from Dirk and Penny found solace. Yet those same two things set her afire with an entirely different result.

Entering her bedroom, she shut the door to the bathroom to keep out the faint sounds coming from Penny's room. She didn't want to be tempted to eavesdrop. Victoria dressed swiftly and applied only a minimum of makeup. As she left her room she hesitated and glanced at her sister's door. After another second's indecision, she walked over and tried the door knob. It was still locked.

She bit at her lips and rapped lightly on the door. "Penny?"

There was a long pause before her sister managed a husky answer. "Yes."

Now what? "W-will you be coming down for dinner?" Two sets of footsteps began climbing the stairs. Victoria turned to see her parents come into view.

"Yes, Penny will have dinner with us." It was Dirk who answered for her sister, his raised voice carrying easily through the closed door.

An eyebrow arched quickly as Lena Beaumont sent Victoria a sharply questioning look. "Is Dirk in Penny's bedroom?"

"Yes." Nervously Victoria brushed a strand of hair away from her forehead. "She was upset, and he's been talking to her."

"It seems to me that some progress might have been made," Charles Beaumont remarked to his wife. "If Dirk is playing the 'big brother' part, then Penny might be getting over her infatuation for him."

"True," her mother agreed thoughtfully, then smiled at Victoria. "You were always so much more self-reliant than Penny, but I've often felt that she needed the guidance of an older brother."

"That isn't true," Victoria denied. "When I needed a big brother there wasn't anyone around to play the role so I had to learn to rely on no one but myself." It hadn't taken Victoria long to learn the art of camouflage to hide her vulnerable feelings. Her appearance of self-reliance was mainly a pose to avoid excessive exposure to hurt. "I'm going downstairs."

"We'll be there directly," her mother promised, eyeing Victoria closely as she passed them to descend the stairs. She had heard the serious note in Victoria's otherwise offhand reply and was reassessing the older daughter she thought she knew so well.

In the kitchen the housekeeper was hurrying about, trying to make up for the time she had let slip away. Victoria volunteered her help and Josie sent her into the dining room to set the table. She was positioning the water goblets around the place settings when Penny walked into the room. Her eyelids were still puffy from crying and her cheeks had a freshly washed glow, but her eyes were bright and clear in their regard.

"Tory, I didn't mean those things I said to you. I'm sorry," Penny apologized.

"I know you didn't," Victoria assured her with a quick smile.

"I quessed that you did—" her younger sister smiled self-consciously "—but I wanted to tell you so myself."

"You were hurt and wanted to hurt back. I know what it's like."

"I'm sorry. I feel better for saying it," Penny shrugged with vague embarrassment.

"I'm sorry too," Victoria offered. Slowly it dawned on her that while Penny might have wanted to make this apology, she had been prompted into doing it by Dirk. Victoria resented his part in this.

"Want some help?" Penny volunteered.

"Uhh . . . no," Victoria refused with a vague shake of her head. "Josie has everything in hand and I'm almost finished here."

"Okay," she nodded and turned to wander aimlessly out of the room.

Sighing, Victoria finished setting out the water goblets and returned to the kitchen for the condiments. She hadn't meant it to sound like a rejection. It wasn't until Penny had left the dining room that it had occurred to Victoria that her sister might have wanted an excuse to stay and talk. As she reentered the dining room carrying the twin sets of salt and pepper shakers,

Dirk walked in. While she tried to maintain an outward show of composure, her nerves were honed to a sharp edge of awareness.

"Have you seen Penny?" he inquired.

"Yes, she was here a minute ago." Victoria set a pair of salt and pepper shakers at one end of the table and had to walk to the opposite end with the remaining pair, which brought her close to where Dirk was standing.

"Did she talk to you?"

Feeling his narrowed look, Victoria didn't meet it. "Yes, and she took back everything she said and apologized. Am I supposed to thank you for that?" The baiting question was an automatic defense mechanism that Victoria couldn't control. Since she couldn't be indifferent to him she was subconsciously trying to erect a barrier of animosity.

"What is this?" He grabbed at her arm and Victoria glanced pointedly at the hand that imprisoned her in its grip.

"What?" She feigned cool innocence.

Dirk swore under his breath, his lips compressing into a thin line. "I knew I shouldn't have given you time to repair that break in your shell."

"I don't know what you're talking about," Victoria insisted.

"That wall of reserve you hide behind. I have to keep cracking open this brittle shell you enclose yourself in. One of these times I'm going to shatter it into so many pieces you won't be able to put it together again," he threatened.

He could, too. But for now it remained in place. "Josie needs my help in the kitchen, would you mind?" She glanced again at the hand that restrained her. Dirk released her and she returned smoothly into the kitchen where she could lick her wounds in relative privacy.

AFTER DINNER, Josie refused her help in washing up and shooed her out of the kitchen into the living room where the others were having coffee. A cushion on the sofa beside Penny was vacant and Victoria immediately took it. It wasn't exactly ideal since she was facing Dirk, seated in an armchair. His hard gaze probed every time it rested on her until she felt like a pin cushion. Victoria didn't taste the coffee she drank, but it kept her from participating in the conversation.

"What's your opinion about the energy situation, Tory?" Dirk unexpectedly directed his question at her.

"I don't discuss political issues," she reminded him.

"I didn't ask you to discuss it. I merely asked your opinion," he challenged with a quirking brow.

She hesitated a fraction of a second, covering it by placing her cup on its saucer. "I have heard my father say—"

Dirk never allowed her to complete it. "Charles, you may have spent a lot of money for her college education, but somewhere along the way someone forgot to teach her to think for herself."

"And someone neglected to inform you that a guest shouldn't be rude!" Victoria flared in retaliation.

"Tory," her mother murmured in a quiet reminder of her own manners.

"No, don't suppress it," Dirk insisted. "If you're angry, let it out," he urged.

Penny frowned. "Why are you two fighting?"

"We aren't fighting." Victoria controlled her temper with an effort. She set her cup and saucer on the coffee table. "Would you excuse me? I have to wash my hair for Mrs. Bourns's party."

"It's difficult to fight when your opponent keeps running, Penny," Dirk observed.

As she flashed him a silvery glare she encountered the curious look her parents exchanged. Admittedly she was running, but it was preferable to being cornered. She escaped into the foyer and ascended the stairs to her bedroom.

Within seconds Penny was knocking at her door. "What's the matter, Tory? Why did you leave?" she questioned.

"I told you. I have to fix my hair for the party tomorrow," Victoria repeated, an excuse that was valid, but it was a task she could have easily accomplished the next morning.

"Why are you so angry with Dirk?" she persisted.

"He was rude."

"I thought you and he were—"

"Well, you thought wrong!" Victoria interrupted sharply and Penny drew back to frown at her. "I'm sorry, I didn't mean to snap."

"If I thought I had any kind of chance at all with him, I'd be downstairs trying to figure out how to be alone with him. Are you scared, Tory?" Penny guessed.

Her mouth opened to vigorously deny it, but she said, "I don't want to talk about it. Would you mind? I'd . . . like to be alone."

Her sister hesitated, then shrugged. "Sure." She backed up toward the door. "I'll be in my room if you change your mind."

"Thanks."

When Penny left Victoria sat on the edge of her bed and stared at the floor. The truth was that she wished she was downstairs with Dirk, alone. He had her so mixed up that she didn't know what she wanted anymore unless it was the peace she had known before he had entered her life.

DRAPING THE MACRAME SHAWL around her shoulders, Victoria adjusted the long tan fringes to hang straight against the cinnamon-colored material of her dress. Since the party was formal, she'd styled her hair in a sophisticated coil that emphasized the classic perfection of her features. Satisfied with the results the mirror reflected, she crossed her bedroom to the door. As she stepped into the upstairs foyer, Dirk came out of his room. His gaze swept over her appearance not missing a single detail.

"You'll dazzle them," he concluded but on a

caustic note. "The party gives you a perfect excuse to parade your diamonds, doesn't it?"

The diamond-studded earrings happened to be the only jewelry she was wearing. They had been a gift from her parents on her twenty-first birthday. She treasured them because of their sentimental value, not their monetary worth, which was probably considerable. It was typical of Dirk to stress the latter.

In an effort to return the barbed compliment, Victoria gave him a raking look. Resplendent in black, Dirk wore the formal attire with casual ease. Instead of looking more civilized, he looked more dangerous.

"You look stunning yourself," she remarked. "You're lucky, rented tuxedos generally don't fit that well."

Her gibe drew a throaty chuckle from him. "You are still trying to put me in my place, aren't you?" Dirk mocked. "Would you like to pretend I'm your chauffeur? I understand heiresses often have affairs with their drivers."

"You have seen too many movies," she retorted.

"By the way, the tux happens to be my own. It comes in handy when I have to lecture at a formal dinner," he explained, a wicked light glinting in his dark eyes. "Luckily I brought it along. Too bad I had to disappoint you by not renting one."

"I'm not disappointed," Victoria replied coolly. "Since we seem to be explaining things, the earrings were a birthday present from my parents.''

"I didn't think they came from an admirer."

"Why not?" she demanded.

"As inhibited as you are I can't imagine you being that seriously involved with someone."

"There is a great deal you don't know about me," Victoria murmured tightly.

"But I intend to find it out," Dirk warned and offered her his arm. "I believe they are waiting for us downstairs. I heard the carriage drive up just before I came out."

She let her hand rest on the black material of his sleeve as they descended the stairs together. Her parents were waiting in the foyer along with Penny and a girl friend she had asked to keep her company while they attended the party.

Since the horse-drawn cab was waiting for them outside, the goodbyes were hurried. Within minutes Victoria was seated beside Dirk in the carriage. A purpling twilight was spreading across the sky, the first star winking down at them.

"It's going to be a lovely night," her mother remarked.

"Yes, it is," Dirk agreed and shifted to curve a possessive arm around Victoria's shoulders. She stiffened, then forced herself to relax in feigned unconcern.

CHAPTER NINE

USING THE STANDARDS SET by previous parties given by Daphne Bourns, this one was small consisting of roughly twenty couples. While it was less crowded, it didn't seem less noisy. The minute they walked in they were swept into the tide of the event.

Daphne attempted to introduce Dirk around, but her obligation as hostess soon called her away, and Victoria's father finished the task. Dirk's arm remained firmly around her waist, taking her with him to whatever cluster of guests her father led him to meet. Other than stating he was a guest and identifying him as a journalist to those who didn't recognize the name, her father didn't offer any more. But the determined way he kept Victoria beside him started the gossips' tongues wagging.

A uniformed caterer finally caught up with them toward the end of the introductions and offered them a glass of champagne from the silver tray he carried. Dirk refused, but Victoria took a glass. She sipped the bubbly wine as a substitute for talking, offering a smile or a nod in acknowledgement of the conversation buzzing around her. Under those conditions it didn't take long to empty the glass. A second caterer was there with a towel-wrapped bottle of champagne to fill it.

"Do you plan on getting drunk?" Dirk inquired, bending his head slightly toward her in an attitude that suggested intimate conversation to any onlookers, of which there were many.

"Wouldn't it meet with your approval if I did?" she challenged over the rim of the glass.

"It might make you more amenable," he conceded, "but, no, I wouldn't approve."

"Amenable, ha!" Victoria drank half of the wine in the shallow glass, nearly choking on the tickling bubbles. "Why don't you join me instead of criticizing all the time?"

"I prefer to get drunk on the sight of you." His gaze ran over her faintly golden features with caressing thoroughness.

Her heart did a crazy tattoo against her ribs as she tried to mock his comment. "Really, that's a terrible line. It reeks of an old Hollywood movie."

"I always thought it did, too," Dirk agreed softly. "But after meeting you I've changed my mind."

"You don't expect me to believe that," she taunted.

"Why not? You remind me of liquor with your whiskey-light hair and the clouded ice of your eyes. A fine aged whiskey from an old bourbon family," he continued with a glinting light in his dark eyes. "The first contact with you leaves the impression of something tall and cool, but one taste and you burn all the way down, Tory.''

She looked away from his compelling male features. ''I've never given anybody indigestion before.'' She was beginning to feel warm all over, but she forced a cool smile onto her lips.

''I don't think an alcoholic would consider the craving to be indigestion,'' Dirk taunted. ''Besides, it's the lingering hangovers that I have trouble with.''

His provocative insinuations were becoming more than she could handle. Across the room, Victoria spied a familiar face and immediately grasped at the straw of escape it offered.

''There's a girl across the way I went to college with, excuse me.'' She tried to move swiftly away.

''I'll come with you. I'd like to meet her,'' he stated.

''I'd rather you didn't,'' Victoria protested.

At that moment her father came to her rescue. ''Dirk, would you come over here a minute?'' he called to him from an adjoining group. ''There's a gentleman here I'd like you to meet.''

When Dirk hesitated, triumph glittered in her gray eyes. ''Go, there might be a marvelous story there for your column.''

Her father glanced at her with a teasing smile. ''Stop monopolizing the man, Tory.'' And it was entirely the other way around.

''I wouldn't dream of it,'' she murmured tightly and nodded to Dirk before she weaved her way through the guests to the brunette she had seen minutes ago. A sixth sense told her Dirk hadn't followed. Before regret could set in she was being greeted by her old classmate.

"Tory! It's been ages!"

"How are you, Racine?" She hugged the slender brunette. "I didn't know you were going to be here."

"Paul and I just came up for the weekend. We're leaving Sunday." Racine Dalbert glanced across the room, her brown eyes shining in quiet speculation. "Who is that stunning man you were with?"

"Dirk Ramsey, a guest of my father's," Victoria replied.

"He looked more like your guest," her friend teased. "Gawd, but he's a handsome devil!"

"Is that any way for a bride of less than a year to talk?" she laughed brittlely.

"If Paul can look and admire a beautiful woman, I'm certainly going to give men like your friend the eye," Racine declared.

"I heard you bought a new house," Victoria changed the subject. "Have you redecorated it all yet?"

"I've tried," the vivacious woman admitted with an exaggerated impish look.

"What's it like? How many rooms?" she prompted.

Victoria sipped her champagne while Racine Dalbert began a lengthy description of her new home and the changes she had made. The conversation naturally led to the adjustments, mostly humorous, of married life. Dodging the question Racine directed at her Victoria kept her college friend talking. The champagne glass was emptied, but the caterer came around with a new tray and Victoria exchanged her empty glass for a full one.

She had barely taken two sips from it when it was taken out of her hand and offered to the brunette. There had been no warning of Dirk's approach until she saw him beside her. Her heart thumped wildly in reaction.

"Would you take this?" He forced the glass into Racine's hand. "Thank you. Excuse us, won't you?"

When the hand at her waist attempted to guide her away, Victoria resisted. "Dirk, this is my friend Racey Dalbert . . . Dirk Ramsey."

"Racey?" His eyebrow arched in questioning amusement.

"Short for Racine," the brunette explained with a throaty laugh. "In my single days it was considered a description." She flirted openly and without embarrassment. "This is the first time I've regretted being out of circulation."

"Racey," he repeated and eyed Victoria. "What did they call you? Miss Conservative?"

"How did you guess?" Racine laughed in surprise. "She isn't really, of course. I mean—"

"I know." A lazy smile played with the corners of his mouth. "It was a pleasure meeting you."

"I'll talk to you later," Victoria promised, unable to dispute the pressure of his arm guiding her away.

"What a pair the two of you must have been," Dirk murmured when they were out of the brunette's hearing. "The tortoise and the hare."

"Racine was, of course, the hare," she replied thinly.

"And you were the snapping turtle," he finished.

"Where are you taking me?" she demanded.

But her question was answered before she had finished asking it. Dirk stopped in a dimly lit alcove of the room that was being used for dancing. He turned her easily into his arms and molded her close to his length.

"This is where I've been wanting you all evening." Dirk curved both of her hands around his neck and let his own slide down her arms, momentarily tangling his fingers in the loose weave of her shawl before they slid beneath to spread over her spine.

"Is it?" She felt weak, but she didn't blame the lethargy on the champagne she had consumed. It was caused by his swaying hips and the seductive pressure of his legs brushing against her thighs as they moved to the slow tempo of the music.

"You know it is." His dark head bent to nuzzle the hair near her temple.

That was too much. Victoria fought back the rising lump of excitement in her throat. Her breath was coming much too shallowly, so she took deeper ones to steady her nervous stomach. The action filled her sense with the earthy fragrance of his cologne and his own unique scent. One disturbance was being traded for another of equal potency.

She lifted her head, seeking to dispel the intimacy with conversation. "Why haven't you ever married?"

"I hadn't planned to get married for several years yet, not until after I became more established in my profession and could cut down on the traveling. Why?"

She couldn't meet his level gaze so she looked over his shoulder and shrugged indifferently. "Racine asked me and I didn't know the answer." She fingered the smooth collar of his jacket. "What happens if you fall in love before that time is up?" Victoria realized that she was intensely interested in his answers and tried not to show it.

"Did Racine arouse all this curiosity about my love life?"

"Of course," she lied.

"To answer your question, it would all depend on the girl, wouldn't it?" Dirk countered.

Something in his tone made her glance at him. His gaze seemed to burrow deep inside her and Victoria couldn't risk that kind of penetrating scrutiny, so she looked away again.

"I imagine it would," she agreed diffidently.

"What would happen if you fell in love with a poor man?" he challenged.

Her first reaction was a startled laugh. "What?"

"Is that so impossible?" Dirk questioned, and his gaze made an arcing sweep of the room. "I suppose it is unlikely since you only associate with your peers."

"I wouldn't judge a man by the money he has—or the lack of it," Victoria defended. "If I loved him I wouldn't care if he was rich or poor—or middle-class."

"Every girl has imagined her ideal mate. What's yours?"

It was a question that made Victoria think. "He would be intelligent, have a sense of humor, be gentle and strong." She hesitated, then added, "Most of all, he would love me."

"Anything else?" Dirk prompted. "What about his looks?"

"Do you mean—would he be tall, dark, and handsome?" A phrase that most aptly described him she realized as she flashed him a look through the sweep of her lashes. She succumbed to the urge to prick his arrogant conceit. "Or fair? Frankly, I don't care what he looks like. Handsome doesn't mean anything. Look at you."

His nostrils flared in a sharp breath of anger. "Are you trying to pick a fight?" Dirk accused, unconsciously tightening the circle of his arms to remind her who was stronger.

"Why would I do that?" she blinked innocently.

His mouth thinned into grimness as he suddenly released her to take hold of her wrist. "Let's get some air," he stated and pulled her along with him to a side door.

Too startled to protest, Victoria let herself be carried along. Once outside he released her arm and reached inside his jacket pocket for a cigarette. With a scrape of his thumbnail across a match head, he ignited a flame and carried it to the tip of his cigarette. Shaking out the fire he exhaled a thin stream of smoke and stared into the star-strewn sky. He seemed to have forgotten she was there.

"I think I'll go back inside," she murmured and started to turn away.

"Oh, no, you don't!" His hand snaked out to seize her arm and pull her back. "You aren't going anywhere." Dirk dropped the freshly lit cigarette and crushed it under his heel. With a muffled groan he crushed her to his length, burying his face in her hair. "Don't you realize what you're doing to me?" he muttered savagely. "I've been one big ache since I met you."

The passion in his voice was so raw that Victoria couldn't believe she had aroused it. "No," she attempted to protest it.

"Yes!" he growled and smothered any response with his mouth.

He moved against her lips with harsh demand until they parted as he pressed her ever tighter into his embrace, as if seeking to absorb her body into his own. Victoria was lost to the scorching rush of emotion that swept through her. The exquisite pain of his fierce embrace tingled through every nerve end. While his hands began moving over her body his mouth followed the soft curves of her face.

The urgency of his need immediately became hers and her hands moved convulsively around his neck. The tumult within was a glorious thing, dazzling and brilliant. She arched ever closer to his thrusting length. Her unconditional surrender removed the pent-up anger from his caresses. They were just as demanding, but more deliberate. She felt him take a shuddering breath.

"I want you, Tory," Dirk mouthed the words against her cheek. "I need you." He changed the statement to a more descriptive sentence.

"Yes." Her voice echoed the husky pitch of his, and she was rewarded with a hard, short kiss. His hand slipped between them to cup her breast. It seemed to swell at his touch, straining against the material that confined it. Her heart felt as if it would burst.

Voices and laughter from inside filtered into the night. They both seemed to realize at the same time that anyone walking out the door would see them. By mutual consent, a small space was allowed to come between them as Dirk removed his hand from her breast to let his fingers caress her cheek and neck. The smoldering desire in his dark eyes kept the flames inside her burning hotly.

"Isn't there any place we can have some privacy?" he questioned thickly.

"I don't know where." She shook her head in a rueful negative.

"My God, what I wouldn't give for a car right now!" A smile twitched at his mouth. "What did couples do in the horse and buggy days? It would be hard to make love in a carriage with the driver watching."

"I suppose that's what enclosed buggys were for . . . and barns and haylofts," Victoria whispered.

"Where's the nearest barn?" He brushed his mouth against her lips and pulled away as if unable to be content with just a kiss.

"I have no idea."

"Have you had enough of this party?" he demanded. When she nodded he folded her hand inside the clasp of his. "Then let's get out of here."

"We'd better tell my parents," she reminded him.

"Don't you think they'll guess where we've disappeared?" he mocked, then shrugged. "We'll tell them."

When they returned inside Victoria saw her parents standing together on the edge of a group. They worked their way through the throng of guests to the side of the older couple.

"There you are," her mother smiled and glanced at the two of them in silent speculation.

"We're going to leave now," Victoria explained.

"We'll come with you," her father said. "Your mother and I were just looking for an excuse to leave, but we didn't feel right about leaving the two of you in the lurch." Without giving anyone an opportunity to speak he held up a hand. "You wait here and I'll call a carriage."

Victoria caught the flicker of irritation that flitted across Dirk's expression, but it was the only indication he gave that he wasn't pleased by the turn of events. Her mother sent her a veiled look of apology.

"Let's find Daphne, shall we?" Lena Beaumont suggested.

By the time they had convinced their hostess that they had truly enjoyed the party, the carriage had arrived to take them home. While her father kept up an easy flow of conversation during the ride, her mother seemed to be the only one who noticed that neither Dirk nor Victoria were contributing much. His arm was around her shoulder, absently massaging her bone in a sensual way. Victoria cast a sideways glance at him. How long had she known Dirk? A week? She shivered.

"Cold?" he murmured.

"A little." At least, her feet were, an age-old symptom of second thoughts.

But Dirk took her literally and nestled her more closely against his side. It didn't seem to help, not as much as Victoria thought it would. The carriage stopped in front of the main entrance to the house and Dirk helped her out. When her parents started toward the door Victoria would have followed, but Dirk held her back.

"We'll be in shortly," he told them calmly.

"What?" Her father gave him a blank look before sudden understanding dawned. "Oh, of course. Good night."

"Good night," Victoria responded as Dirk was already guiding her toward the iron gates to the breezeway.

Without speaking he escorted her through them. All the while her mind kept remembering his statement that he had no plans for getting married for several years yet. So what was he offering her in the meantime? An affair? Of what duration? The length of his stay with them? Or maybe he'd stop in to see her whenever he was in the vicinity? Could she be satisfied with such a casual commitment? Her feet were becoming lumps of ice.

Some of the spreading numbness must have crept into her lips because they were coolly unresponsive when he turned her into his arms and covered them with his own. His mouth moved persuasively against them. Her lips softened, but with a weak imitation of their previous yielding. Dirk lifted his head, a gathering frown darkening his expression.

"What's the matter?"

"I don't know. I . . . ." How could she tell him without exposing herself to be hurt? "I think I'd better go inside."

"Victoria?" He caught her shoulders and

stared incredulously into her face. "At the party, you wanted this moment."

"Yes, I know," she admitted.

"Now you don't," he accused.

"I'm not sure."

"My God, first you're hot, then you're cold!" Dirk released her in a burst of irritation. "How do you turn it on and off like water faucets? Will you tell me? I would really like to know. Is it some secret? Because it doesn't work that way with me."

His anger was justified, but it didn't make it sting any less. "Maybe I just want to know where I stand?" Victoria challenged.

"What does that mean?" he demanded. "Do you expect me to get down on my knees and beg for the privilege to make love to you? Am I supposed to swear some undying allegiance? Who does the giving and who does the taking, Victoria? Maybe that's something that I should know, too."

She stared at him wordlessly, a terrible pain shattering through her body. There wasn't anything she could say, so she pivoted toward the sliding glass doors. Again Dirk caught at her arm, but Victoria wouldn't turn around, aware of the tears filling her eyes, and he didn't make her face him.

"Just what the hell do you expect from me?" he declared.

Victoria had to fight to get the word out of her pain-taut throat, but she finally succeeded. "Nothing."

He let her go and she glided across the stone floor to the living-room entrance. Once inside the house, she didn't stop until she had climbed the stairs to her room. She undressed in the dark and fumbled in the closet to hang up her dress. Yanking the pins from her hair, she found the physical pain a welcome counterbalance to the emotional anguish tearing her apart inside. Victoria brushed her hair until her scalp hurt before finally going in search of her nightgown. It eluded her in the dark.

The sound of footsteps mounting the stairs froze her beside the dresser. She didn't make a sound to draw Dirk's attention to her bedroom. Yet his quiet tread approached her door. The knob turned and the door was pushed open. Victoria was unaware that she was framed by the moonlight streaming in through the window. She was only conscious of the dark shadow that loomed in her doorway.

"I'll scream," she threatened in a voice that was lower than a whisper.

If he had said one word to her she probably would have raced into his arms. Instead, his shadow receded and the door swung closed. Rejection rooted her to the floor as Victoria listened to him walk to his room. Silently, she walked to her door and turned the lock. Forgetting the nightgown she hadn't found, she went to her bed and crawled under the covers where she cried silently.

CHAPTER TEN

VICTORIA SPENT LONG, sleepless hours trying to decide whether she had made a mistake. She couldn't make up her mind whether her decision had been right or wrong. Either way, she was convinced she would have experienced the same anguish and doubt.

As a result, she awakened feeling more wretched than she had the night before. A glance in the mirror while she was brushing her teeth revealed that she looked worse than she felt. It took a series of cold water compresses to fade the redness in her eyes and dissolve their puffiness. Heavy makeup hid the rest of the damage from her restless night.

Dressed in a pair of red jeans and a striped top, Victoria was about to leave her room when she heard a carriage stop in front of the house. She glanced out the window as the driver alighted from his seat. Briefly she wondered where her parents were going this morning as she walked out the door.

From the top of the stairs she could see everyone gathered in the foyer below, her parents, Penny, and the housekeeper. Was everyone leaving, she wondered with a frown and started down the steps. Then she saw the luggage stacked beside the door and Dirk shaking hands with her father.

"What's going on?" Her sharp question drew everyone's gaze, including Dirk's. His expression looked as grim as she felt. When she looked into his dark eyes she had the sensation of falling into a black, bottomless well. At the same time it felt as if her heart was plummeting all the way to her toes.

Penny dashed to the bottom of the stairs to meet her. "Dirk is leaving. Won't you tell him he doesn't have to go?" Her confused blue eyes sent a silent appeal for Victoria's support.

Even though the luggage by the door had given her the first clue, to actually hear someone say the thing she had guessed, Victoria felt stunned. Her widened gaze swung back to Dirk. "I thought you were planning to stay another week."

"We all did," her mother agreed. "But he's convinced that he has to leave and we simply haven't been able to talk him out of it."

"You've been very generous with your hospitality, Lena," Dirk smiled, but without warmth. "But I've outstayed my welcome. Haven't I?" The last was issued as a direct challenge to Victoria.

"Have you ever heard such nonsense?" her mother declared, but her eyes were questioning Victoria, asking her the cause.

There was a knock at the door and Victoria was saved from responding. Dirk was the closest to the door. He opened it and Victoria glimpsed the carriage driver standing outside. Dirk sliced a glance at Victoria before speaking to the man.

"I'll be with you in a minute," he said and the driver nodded before moving out of sight. Dirk didn't close the door as he turned to face the others in the foyer. "I'd like to speak to Victoria for a few minutes. Alone, if you don't mind."

"Of course not," her father agreed and quietly shepherded the others into the living room.

When they were alone Dirk looked at her expectantly and waited. "Were you going to leave without saying goodbye?" she demanded in weak defense.

"Penny said you were awake, that you'd be down as soon as you were dressed." Which wasn't really an answer.

"What if I hadn't come down? The carriage had already arrived when I left my room." It hurt to think he would have left without attempting to see her, and she was very vulnerable this morning.

"I would have sent Penny upstairs to tell you I was leaving," Dirk replied.

"Everyone expects you to stay another week."

"What would it accomplish?" he challenged, tipping his head back to eye her.

It was meant as a personal question, but Victoria chose to misinterpret it. "The reason for your visit was to become better acquainted with my father. Isn't that what you hoped to accomplish?"

"I know the reason that I came." He darted an impatient look toward the living room and reached for her hand to draw her behind him out the door. When it was closed he squared around to face her. "Is there any reason why I should stay another week, Tory?"

She hesitated and moved closer to the wood timbers that framed the front door. "We never did play that tennis game to break the tie with my parents," she reminded him nervously. "And you haven't taken a tour of the island. Fort Mackinac is really quite fascinating sitting on those limestone cliffs that overlook the harbor and the Straits of Mackinac. And there's the governor's mansion—it's open to the public."

"Victoria." He cut across her silly chattering, his jaw hardening into bronze.

"Excuse me, sir," the carriage driver interrupted him. "Are you ready to leave?"

"Not yet!" Dirk snapped, then took a deep breath. "I have some luggage inside the door." He pushed the door open. "You might as well load it in the carriage for me."

"Yes, sir." The man moved from the horse's head and walked across the stone entry to the door. Victoria watched him juggle the suitcases, carrying them all in one trip. When he loaded them in the carriage Dirk's departure seemed suddenly very final.

"You really are leaving," she murmured.

"I can have him unload that luggage," Dirk replied.

"Are you going to?" Victoria held her breath.

"Do you want me to stay?" he asked instead. She couldn't answer that. It would be much too revealing. Dirk became impatient with her silence. "A simple yes or no will do."

"I don't know!" she flared in agitation.

"Look, I don't know what you want from me." His gaze resembled sharp blades of black steel cutting into her and slicing her into tiny pieces. "One minute you are practically inviting me into your bed and in the next you are trying to keep me at a respectful distance. I am not going to stay around here and be your yo-yo that you can wind up, then let fall as it suits your fancy. I don't dance on anybody's string."

"I never asked you to. You don't understand," Victoria protested.

"Why don't you try to explain?" Dirk challenged.

"I don't know you!"

"What is it that you want to know?" His hands were lifted palms upward in a beseeching gesture that reflected his exasperation. "I'm male, thirty-four years old, single, a reporter. I like children and a good joke. I smoke, but I don't drink. I play tennis, football, chess, handball, and a couple of other sports. I've never struck a woman in my life, but you are sorely testing me. As far as I know I'm in good health. Maybe you want to check my teeth. Shall I send you my dental records? Sorry I can't supply you with a family tree, but I've never been too concerned about my lineage."

"I don't care about that!" She raked the hair

behind her ears, inwardly wincing at his digging
gibes.

"Then you'll have to be more specific in your
request," he countered, not letting up on his
anger.

"Are you ready yet, sir?" It was the driver
again.

Dirk pivoted to glare at him. "Hold your
horses!" Immediately he released a long sigh.
"Sorry, I wasn't trying to be funny. I'll be there
in a minute." He turned back to Victoria.
"Well?"

"You can't give me an ultimatum like this,"
she protested. "I need more time."

"How much time? Another week?"

"I don't know." She shrugged impatiently.

"What then? Two weeks? A month? A year?
How long is it going to take for you to decide?"
he demanded.

"I can't narrow it down like that!"

"If you can't then I guess you've answered my
question. I've taken my quota of cold showers,
Victoria." The anger was gone from his voice,
leaving it hard and flat. "And I'm not going to
lay awake any more nights thinking about you in
the bedroom across the hall. So I guess this is
goodbye."

"You don't have to go." There were hot tears
stinging the back of her eyes.

Just for an instant Victoria glimpsed a flicker
of regret in his dark eyes. Then his hands were
firmly taking her shoulders and drawing her

toward him. Automatically her head tipped back to meet his descending mouth. His kiss was warm and fiercely gentle. Victoria couldn't believe that Dirk could kiss her like this, with all this leashed hunger, and then leave. Her arms wound around his neck as she arched on her tiptoes to deepen the kiss. His hands slid over her shoulder bones to press her close to his length and the hard male shape of him that was so familiar to her flesh. Just for a minute a flame leaped to consume them both; then Dirk was reaching up to pull her arms from around his neck and set her away.

"All you have to do is ask me to stay," he told her.

She stared at him helplessly, an enormous lump in her throat. With a wry, grimacing smile, Dirk turned away and walked to the carriage. She stood where he had left her, not really believing he would leave. He motioned to the driver who clicked to the horse and tapped his whip on its rump. Dirk was rubbing the back of his neck in a weary gesture as the carriage moved away from the curb. Victoria waited for him to look back at her, but he never did. Some vital part was wrenched from her soul and went with him. She stayed by the door until he was out of sight.

"Dirk, will you stay?" she asked in a voice barely above a whisper, but, of course, he didn't hear her. An icy shudder wracked her body and she hugged her arms around her.

The front door burst open and Penny came flying out. "Couldn't you make him stay?" she moaned.

"No." Her chin quivered in weak betrayal as her eyes became filled with tears.

"Did you ask him?" Penny demanded.

"No," Victoria admitted and turned to walk into the house.

"Has Dirk gone?" her mother inquired when she entered the foyer. Victoria managed a faint nod of affirmation. Her heart silently echoed her mother's sigh of regret. "Your father and I were just going to have our breakfast. Why don't you join us, Tory?"

She shook her head and walked blindly to the stairs, her vision blurred by the gathering tears. "I'm not hungry." Victoria knew the choked tightness of her voice was a betrayal, but she couldn't hide it.

The tears slithered down her cheeks as she climbed the stairs to her room. She sat on the edge of her bed and rocked slowly back and forth, letting the tears fall unchecked.

"If you are crying because he's gone, why didn't you ask him to stay?" Penny frowned, standing in the doorway.

"I couldn't," she managed.

"Why?" Her sister was plainly confused.

Lena Beaumont entered the room. "Tory, are you all right?" She walked to the bed and sat down beside Victoria, putting a comforting arm around her shoulder.

"Yes." The nod of assurance wavered.

"She's crying because Dirk left but she wouldn't ask him to stay," Penny explained.

"Did you want him to stay?" her mother asked.

Victoria lifted her shoulders in an uncertain shrug. "I don't know," she whispered.

"Are you in love with him?"

"I've barely known him a week," she reminded her mother with a tearful laugh.

"Love isn't measured by time, dear. A woman can be married to a man for twenty years and never know him at all. It's just something that happens or doesn't," Lena reasoned.

"How can I be sure?" Victoria shook her head in confusion.

"Love is something you have to take on faith. There are no certainties," she murmured. "Does Dirk love you?"

"I don't know." She wiped at the river of tears swamping her cheeks. "He told me he didn't want to get married for several years yet. So. . . . He cared, but. . . ." She couldn't finish it.

"Are you going to see him again?" Penny asked.

Again Victoria shrugged. "He said goodbye, so I don't suppose I will."

"But he might," her sister offered hopefully. "You said that he cared about you. If he does he'll see you again."

"He said he would stay if I asked him, but I didn't ask," Victoria explained.

"Why?" It was her mother who asked this time.

"Because I don't know if he wanted to stay because I'm Charles Beaumont's daughter or because he cared about me. It's something I don't think you understand, mom," she said tightly.

"I do," Penny spoke up. "Millie van Bolten used to be my best friend. Do you know why? Because we have a tennis court at our house. That's the only reason she always wanted to come over."

"You've learned that, too, have you?" Victoria exchanged a sad smile with her sister.

"Who needs Millie van Bolten?" Penny shrugged.

"Who needs Dirk Ramsey?" Victoria copied the gesture, but she knew the two didn't compare. She may have only known him a week, but it would be a long time before she got over him.

CHAPTER ELEVEN

THE CITY STREET was lined with shabby brick buildings and their cobweb of rusty fire escapes, and sets of concrete steps leading from the sidewalk to the individual entrances. Victoria parked her car at the curb, slipping the strap of her purse over her shoulder before reaching for the bag of groceries on the passenger seat.

When she stepped out of the car a blustery autumn wind whipped a section of yesterday's newspaper against her leg, then chased it down the street. Locking the door, she shut it and walked around the hood to the cracked cement walk with its tufts of brown grass growing through the fissures. The sky was leaden and depressing, its dull gray color doing nothing to uplift the tedious row of apartment buildings.

Carrying the grocery bag in front of her Victoria started toward the building in the center of the block. It was easily distinguishable from the others since it was the only one with a hand rail on the concrete steps.

"Hey there, Queenie! What 'cha doin'?" A young male voice hailed her from across the street.

A half smile was already curving her mouth when she turned. "Hi, Rick," she greeted the

youth jogging across the street toward her.
Another boy was with him but Victoria didn't
know him. She smiled at him, anyway.

"Long time no see," Rick declared, stopping
in front of her. His hand flicked out to touch the
grocery bag. "Ya on your way to granny's
house."

"Yes, I'm running a little late though. Mrs.
Ogden has probably given up on me," she
sighed.

"Who's Mrs. Ogden?" the other boy asked.

"Ah, you know her. The old lady that lives
downstairs from me," Rick informed him with
little patience. "Queenie, this is my friend Fred.
Fred, this is Queenie. She brings granny her
groceries 'cause she's too crippled to leave the
apartment."

"Hello, Fred." Victoria acknowledged the introduction with a nod.

"'lo," he mumbled, eyeing her uncertainly,
but she was used to being regarded with suspicion in this neighborhood.

"Shouldn't you boys be in school?" She
frowned as she happened to glance at her watch
and noticed it was still very early in the afternoon.

"Naw, we got ourselves expelled," Rick
replied in a faintly bragging tone.

"Yeah, by the big man hisself," his friend added.

"What kind of trouble did you get into this

time?'' Victoria asked, since it was an occurrence that seemed to happen about once a month.

"The big man, he conducted hisself a little illegal search and seizure,'' Rick explained. He could speak excellent English, but when he was with his friends he used the language of the street.

"Yeah, and when he happen to find a knife like this one—'' the boy named Fred proudly flashed a switchblade "—he expelled us.''

"I thought you said he took yours,'' Victoria reminded him.

Rick took one from his pocket and snapped it open. "We just got ourselves another.'' He shrugged, then eyed his friend and laughed.

"A fella needs protection,'' Fred laughed.

"What you get is trouble,'' Victoria replied.

"You got yourself trouble,'' Rick said, gesturing at her with his knife. "I don't remember you bein' so skinny. How come you work so hard when you don't have to?''

"To keep from being bored,'' she answered rather than admit it was to keep her mind occupied with something other than thoughts of Dirk Ramsey. Yet working hadn't helped her appetite or let her fall asleep any quicker at night, which was the longest part of any day.

"Man! If I had that car—'' Fred pointed to hers "—I sure wouldn't be bored.''

"Ain't that the truth.'' Rick began cleaning

under his fingernails with the pointed end of the switchblade knife.

"I'd better get up to Mrs. Ogden's before this milk starts to sour," she stated.

"Me and Fred better go along with you. We got some punks that moved onto the block. They ain't learned their manners, yet," Rick explained.

"I'd like the company," she agreed.

Brakes squealed as a shiny black sports car swerved to a stop at the curb near them. Shock drained the color from her face when she saw Dirk step quickly out of the car and come swiftly around the hood to the sidewalk.

"What are you doing here, Dirk?" she asked in disbelief. Not a word from him in three months and to have him show up on this particular street was stretching coincidence too far.

"I was in town so I called your parents to say hello." Other than a brief assessing look at her wan face, his gaze hadn't left the two young men eyeing him so warily. "Your mother mentioned that she had expected you back an hour ago. When she gave me this address I realized why she sounded worried."

"As you can see, I'm all right," Victoria frowned, feeling a twinge of rejection in his attitude. He didn't appear interested at all in seeing her again. He'd only come to soothe her mother's needless fears.

He slipped a hand under her elbow. "Just the same, you're coming with me."

"No, I'm not." She shrugged her arm out of his grasp and took a step away.

"I don't want to argue with you, Tory," Dirk said flatly.

"The lady don't have to go with you if she don't want to," Rick inserted. "She's got business here."

"You just put those knives away and butt out," Dirk warned.

"Hey! He wants us to put our knives away," Fred laughed.

"Maybe he's worried about gettin' that handsome face of his all cut up," Rick joined in.

"Don't try it, guys." Every nerve was alert. Victoria saw the ruthless line of Dirk's mouth and knew he meant it.

"I think he's threatening us." Fred took a step backward in mock fear.

"Maybe we should do a little threatening of our own, huh?" Rick waved his blade in front of him. Victoria had known Rick for almost three years. She could tell by the mischievous light in his eyes that he was only teasing. Her concern was only for the embarrassment he was causing himself with such juvenile behavior. Rick make a swipe with his knife toward Dirk, but it was a swing that was intended to be short of its mark. Instead of stepping backward to avoid the sharp blade, Dirk stepped in behind it and grabbed the boy's wrist, twisting it behind his back and hooking an elbow around Rick's throat all in one motion. The knife clattered to the pavement. Rick clawed at the muscled arm.

"Hey man! You gonna break my neck!" he protested hoarsely.

"Let him go, Dirk," Victoria added her pleas to the boy's. "He didn't mean any harm."

"We was just funnin'," Fred insisted, folding his knife closed and backing off.

When Dirk released the boy he pushed him forward to sprawl on the sidewalk. Watching both of them carefully, he reached down and picked up the knife that had fallen. He snapped it shut, but held it for another instant.

"On my street, you never flashed a knife unless you were going to use it. You'd better keep that in mind the next time, *man*," Dirk advised and tossed the closed knife to Rick. He sliced a glance at Victoria. "Are you ready to come with me?"

"I have to take these groceries up to Mrs. Ogden's. She lives in that middle building," she retorted.

"Okay, then I'm coming with you." His hand slid under her elbow again as he took a step then paused to glance at the youths sidling away from him. "Is this your turf?"

"Yeah," Rick admitted with faint defiance as he rubbed his arm and flexed it.

Dirk took a bill from his pocket and handed it to him. "Watch my car. I wouldn't like to come back and find the tires slashed."

"You got it!" the boy grinned.

"All right. Now let's go." He ushered her forward to the set of steps with the handrail. He glanced at the street number painted above the row of mailboxes. "Your father owns this building, doesn't he? I seem to remember the address when I did some background work on him."

"Yes, he does," Victoria retorted defensively. "You'll find that all the electrical wiring is new, the plumbing works as well as the furnace."

"I know." There was a lazy curve to his mouth that told her he'd already verified that several months ago. "Who's the punk? One of your secret admirers?"

"Do you mean Rick? He lives in the building. Since I've started stopping by to see Mrs. Ogden, we've become friends," she explained. "He really wasn't going to hurt you."

"He didn't look very friendly when I drove up." Dirk opened the main door to the building and held it for her.

"Did you think they were assaulting me?" The possibility just occurred to her.

"The sight of two street toughs stopping a beautiful woman on a sidewalk just to show her their knives is not very common," he reminded her dryly. "Which floor is your lady friend on?"

"The second one," she answered. "That is what Rick was doing—showing me his knife," she elaborated. "The principal expelled them from school for carrying them."

As she led the way up the steps, Victoria realized that they were both behaving as if it hadn't been three months since they'd last seen each other. Yet there was a new feeling present that she hadn't known before—the sensation of being protected.

Several weeks ago she had accepted the fact that she was in love with him, but since he'd made no effort to get in touch with her she had decided it was one-sided. Seeing him again was reinforcing the emotion and giving her a thread of hope that it wasn't unrequited. Suddenly she had an attack of nerves.

"How . . . have you been?" She darted him a guarded look and noticed there were more hard lines cut into his features and the hollows under his cheekbones seemed leaner.

His gaze touched her briefly, but he didn't answer the question. "Which apartment is hers?"

"The second one on the right." She stood to one side while he knocked on it.

"Who is it?" Mrs. Ogden's aging voice cracked in demand.

"It's me, Victoria," she answered.

The whir of a wheelchair being propelled forward by a motor filtered into the narrow hallway. Then there was some fumbling with the locks before the knob turned and the door was swung inward.

"I'm sorry I'm late, but Mrs. Jackson wasn't well," Victoria explained.

But the woman waved her explanation aside with a gnarled hand. "Who is this young man?"

Although her voice cracked occasionally and her fingers were crippled with arthritis, her blue eyes sparkled with a fountainous wealth of youth. Her hair was snow-white and her flawless complexion had always reminded Victoria of bone china.

"This is Dirk Ramsey, a friend of mine," she introduced. "Dirk, this is Mrs. Ogden."

The woman added to her own introduction, "A very old lady who was afraid she was going to wait an eternity before she finally met Victoria's young man."

"It's my pleasure, Mrs. Ogden." Dirk bowed slightly as he bent to shake her hand.

"Oh, he's very handsome, Victoria," she smiled.

"Yes, he is," she agreed, wondering if she should have contradicted the impression Mrs. Ogden had formed about Dirk's relationship to her.

"Do you know that is the first time Victoria has ever admitted that I was handsome?" Dirk observed with a glinting look at her. "I'm going to have to come with Victoria to visit you more often, Mrs. Ogden."

"I would like that," the woman beamed under his smile. His charm knew no age limit, it seemed.

"I'll put the groceries away for you," Victoria murmured and turned toward the cubbyhole room that served as a kitchen in the small apartment.

"Let Dirk put them away. It's good practice for a man," Mrs. Ogden instructed.

"Oh, I . . . ." Victoria started to protest, certain he would never agree to it, but Dirk had already reached out and was taking the bag of groceries out of her arms.

"I don't mind," he murmured, leaving her a little disconcerted as he carried the groceries into the kitchen.

"Come with me, Victoria." Mrs. Ogden pivoted her chair and guided it to the open space by the window where she usually positioned her chair during the day. "I have something for you."

A little confused Victoria glanced toward the kitchen, wondering whether Dirk would put the supplies where the woman could easily find them. She would simply have to double-check before she left. She followed the woman across the room. Mrs. Ogden was trying to unfasten the looped clasp of her large, wicker sewing basket.

"Let me open it for you," Victoria offered and knelt beside the basket.

She had always marveled that the woman had continued her sewing, a task that had to be difficult as well as painful considering the gnarled stiffness of her fingers. But Mrs. Ogden insisted that sewing had kept her hands fairly nimble, besides bringing her enjoyment during the long, lonely hours in the apartment.

"Do you see that bundle near the bottom wrapped in tissue?" The woman pointed. "Would you hand it to me?"

"Of course." The thin paper crackled as Victoria slipped it out from beneath the skeins of yarn and half-finished Afghans. She placed it on the woman's lap, and waited while Mrs. Ogden began to painstakingly unwrap it.

"I started crocheting this two days after you visited me for the first time. That was nearly three years ago, remember?"

"Yes, I certainly do," Victoria nodded.

"Every girl should have a fancy tablecloth when she gets married, or so my mother claimed," Mrs. Ogden winked. "So I started making this for you, but I fully expected you to be married before I finished. Your timing was excellent because I only completed it last week."

"You made this for me?" Victoria repeated with a questioning frown. Even as she said it, the last layer of tissue paper was carefully folded away to reveal the tiny, precise stitches that formed the wild-rose-designed, crocheted tablecloth.

"Yes, it's for you," Mrs. Ogden confirmed and lifted the tablecloth free of the paper to hand it to her.

Victoria held it gently, fingering the delicate threads that formed the intricate pattern. When she thought of the time, the labor, the pain it had cost the woman to crochet this for her, she was overwhelmed. Tears sprang to her eyes as she glanced at the gnarled hand on the armrest of the wheelchair. Bending, she kissed the crippled fingers, then pressed her cheek against them.

"Thank you," she whispered and felt the light, stroking caress of Mrs. Ogden's other hand on her hair. "I'll invite you to my first dinner party," Victoria promised as she lifted her head to gaze into the sparkling blue eyes.

"Gracious, no!" Mrs. Ogden laughed. "I'll knock something over with these awkward hands of mine and stain it."

"Your hands aren't awkward," Victoria insisted, spreading her smooth and supple hand over the bony appendage on the armrest. "Hands that could create something as beautiful as this could never be awkward."

"That is a lovely thing to say. Thank you, Victoria."

There was a flicker of movement out of the corner of her eye. Victoria turned her head slightly to see Dirk standing in the arched opening to the tiny kitchen. His look was gently questioning. Self-consciously, she wiped the damp film of tears from her cheeks and straightened, carefully holding the handmade tablecloth.

"Mrs. Ogden made this for me," she explained.

He moved forward to touch the slender threads hooked so closely together to make the wild-rose pattern. His gaze skimmed her overly bright gray eyes, then slid to the woman in the chair.

"It's lovely work, Mrs. Ogden. No wonder Victoria is so proud." It wasn't a patronizing statement, issued to be polite. Dirk sounded as if he truly meant every single word he said. Victoria wanted to hug him.

"I don't have any children of my own to do these things for," the woman murmured with a trace of poignancy. "Both of my sons were killed in the war. They had no children. So I don't have any grandchildren except the ones I adopt, like Victoria."

"Why don't you let me fix you some coffee?" Victoria suggested.

"No, you and your young man I'm sure would like to be alone. I know how that is. I'm just pleased you brought him along so I could meet him." There was a glimmer of tears in the woman's eyes, but she determinedly blinked them away. "You two run along."

"I would like to have a cup of coffee with you, Mrs. Ogden," Dirk insisted.

"Liar," she teased gruffly. "You'd like to have that girl beside you all to yourself. Come see me another time."

"We can't fool you, can we?" Dirk smiled.

"Indeed, you can't! Now, shoo! Both of you!" She waved them out of the apartment.

"Just let me check to be certain Dirk put everything where you can reach it," Victoria insisted and pressed the cloth into his hands as she hurried into the kitchen. Surprisingly, everything was exactly where it belonged. When she came back in, Dirk had rewrapped the tablecloth in the protective tissue paper and he handed it back to her. Before leaving she bent and kissed the woman on the cheek. "Thank you again."

"I'll talk to you tomorrow," Mrs. Ogden smiled.

In the hallway Dirk waited for her as she closed the door. "Does she call you?" he asked.

"Actually I call her. Either myself or another woman phones every day to be certain she's all right and that there isn't anything that she needs," Victoria explained. "When I first started visiting her I tried to persuade her to move out. But she's lived in this building practically all of her life. It's her home. I'm just grateful that she has a front apartment so she can see out."

Dirk paused at the bottom of the stairs and looked up the dark stairwell. "My mother wouldn't move out of our old apartment building, either. She died there. Unfortunately she didn't have anyone like you who checked on her every day and kept her company—not even me," he admitted with a bitter twist of his mouth.

"You weren't living there?"

"No, I was going to college and working." He shrugged and reached in front of her to open the door. "It was a long time ago." Her hand smoothed the tissue paper that covered the tablecloth and Dirk noticed the action. "You like that, don't you?"

"Yes." Victoria expected him to mock her reasons, but he simply gave her a gentle look that melted her wariness. "It's actually a wedding gift."

"I know." His hand rested lightly on the back of her waist as they walked down the concrete steps to the sidewalk.

"I didn't have the heart to correct her when she thought you and I were getting married," she apologized.

"Neither did I." Dirk looked straight ahead toward his car and the boys waiting beside it. "We'll work it out later." As they neared his car he asked, "Do either of you have a current driver's license?"

"I do," Rick said and pulled a slim wallet out of his hind pocket to show him.

Dirk wrote something on a slip of paper and handed it to Rick along with a set of car keys. "Take my car to this address, and no joyriding," he warned.

"Do you mean it?" Rick eyed him suspiciously. "The car ain't hot, is it?"

"Yes, I mean it, and no, it isn't stolen. Now get going."

Rick let out a whoop and raced around to the driver's door. "Can Fred come along?"

"You just remember what I said about no joyriding, and I don't care who rides with you as long as the car is in the same condition it's in now," Dirk replied.

"Aren't you taking a chance to trust them with your car?" Victoria murmured.

"If you were safe with them, I think my car is.

You and I are going for a little drive. We have some things to talk about." He held out his hand for the keys to her car and Victoria gave them to him, a tiny thread of excitement weaving through her nerve ends.

CHAPTER TWELVE

HOPE WAS FLITTING ABOUT her shoulders as Dirk slid behind the wheel and started the car. There seemed so few subjects that he would want to talk to her about, but Victoria contained her curiosity until he identified the topic. He waited until he had driven away from the curb and into city traffic.

"I lied to you," he stated.

"When? About what?" The startled questions sprang from her.

"When I said I happened to be in town and called your parents out of courtesy. That was a lie. I canceled in the middle of a lecture tour to fly here. And I didn't call to talk to your parents—I wanted to speak to you."

"Why?" She held her breath, crossing her fingers beneath the cover of the tissue paper.

"Because I've had all the sleepless nights I can stand. We've got to work out a compromise." Dirk kept his gaze fixed on the traffic, a muscle working convulsively in his jaw. "I don't know how long it's going to take for you to get to know me better, but I think I can understand some of the apprehensions you had."

"I'm glad because—"

"No, hear me out," he interrupted. "When we're married, I have asked your father to disinherit you. If he wants to set up a trust fund administered by his people to take care of you in the event of my death, or for our children, I have no objection. But I don't want you to ever think that I have any interest in your money."

An incredulous joy trembled through her. Not only did he want to marry her, but he was also denouncing any claim to her inheritance. It was more than she had hoped for, more than she had dared to dream.

"Unless you want the fanfare of a big wedding, I would just as soon be married in a chapel. You've lived in a goldfish bowl long enough. The only notoriety you are going to have from now is being the wife of Dirk Ramsey."

"Dirk, would you stop the car?" Her voice wavered on a breathless note of sheer happiness.

"Not yet. I'll have to cut down on my traveling, but I've found a house in the country convenient to Washington, D. C. It needs some fixing up, but I think we can do it. There won't be any housekeeper, not for awhile anyway. You can continue to call Mrs. Ogden as long as the long-distance phone calls don't become absurdly expensive. Have I left anything out?" he murmured, as if to himself.

"I hope I'm going to have a baby," Victoria inserted.

"What?" His head jerked around to stare at her.

"Watch where you're going," she warned.

Dirk had to slam on the brakes and swerve into the next lane to avoid the car turning in front of them. A horn blared and brakes squealed behind them.

"What possessed you to say such a thing?" he demanded, taking a deep breath.

"You seemed to have everything else planned, but you didn't mention anything about children. I'd like to have one or two." A tiny smile tugged at the corners of her mouth. "Have you picked out my ring? I hope it's something simple. I'm not much for flashy jewelry."

"Wait a minute. What are you saying?" Suddenly he was the one who was uncertain.

"I think we were talking about getting married, weren't we?" she teased. "There's a parking spot over there." She pointed to a meter by the curb two car lengths ahead of them.

Dirk quickly maneuvered the car into the parking place and switched off the motor. As he turned in the seat to face her, Victoria had the impression he was straining toward her even though he hadn't moved.

"You want to marry me . . . with no arguments?"

"No arguments," she agreed. Before she finished the movement that took her toward him, Dirk was reaching out to gather her into his arms.

The hunger that had been bottled up from long months apart was appeased in a long, aching kiss. It was followed by a shower of smaller ones that they rained over each other's features. Victoria felt the violent shudder that quaked through his body, and understood its cause.

"I thought I'd lost you," she whispered. "Everything happened so fast. I was so scared, so unsure. I thought love was something that had to grow, not just suddenly explode on the horizon one day."

"Nobody ever tied me up in knots the way you did," Dirk insisted. "I never gave you a chance to think. I had to learn patience. I had to leave you to find out I couldn't live without you. I don't want to live without you."

"You said marriage wasn't part of your plans," Victoria reminded him.

"I said that it hadn't been part of my plans, but my plans had been undergoing revisions since the day I saw you—that gorgeous rich girl, pampered, spoiled, only you weren't any of those things. If I needed any proof of that, you gave it to me today crying over a tablecloth some old woman made."

"It's the love, the caring that she crocheted in every stitch," Victoria attempted to explain.

"You don't have to tell me," he laughed softly and kissed her.

"Dirk, have you checked to find out how long it will take to get a license and a minister?"

"Not yet, but you'd better believe it's the first thing I'm going to do," he promised. "I'm not going to give you a chance to change your mind."

"I'm not going to change my mind. When that carriage disappeared I finally realized that I loved you," she admitted.

"Why didn't you write? Or call?" he groaned and rubbed his cheeks against her hair.

"I didn't think you loved me."

His mouth found hers to do whatever convincing that still needed to be done.

For the millions who can't read
Give the Gift of Literacy

One out of five adults in North America
cannot read or write well enough
to fill out a job application
or understand the directions on a bottle of medicine.

You can change all this by joining the fight
against illiteracy.

For more information write to:
Contact, Box 81826, Lincoln, Neb. 68501
In the United States, call toll free: 800-228-3225

The only degree you need
is a degree of caring

Six exciting series for you every month... from Harlequin

Harlequin Romance·
The series that started it all

Tender, captivating and heartwarming...
love stories that sweep you off to faraway places
and delight you with the magic of love.

◆

Harlequin Presents·
Powerful contemporary love stories...as individual as the women who read them

The No. 1 romance series...
exciting love stories for you, the woman of today...
a rare blend of passion and dramatic realism.

◆

Harlequin Superromance®
It's more than romance... it's Harlequin Superromance

A sophisticated, contemporary romance-fiction
series, providing you with a longer,
more involving read...a richer mix of complex plots,
realism and adventure.

Harlequin
American Romance
Harlequin celebrates the American woman...

...by offering you romance stories written
about American women, by American women
for American women. This series offers you
contemporary romances uniquely North American
in flavor and appeal.

◆

Harlequin Temptation
Passionate stories for today's woman

An exciting series of sensual, mature stories of
love...dilemmas, choices, resolutions...
all contemporary issues dealt with in a true-to-life
fashion by some of your favorite authors.

◆

Harlequin Intrigue
Because romance can be quite an adventure

Harlequin Intrigue, an innovative series that
blends the romance you expect...
with the unexpected. Each story has an added
element of intrigue that provides a new twist to
the Harlequin tradition of romance excellence.

GILLIAN HALL

The magnificent novel of a woman
fighting for her greatest passion—
and for a love to fulfill
her deepest desires.

The desire to break from an unbearable past takes prima ballerina
Anna Duras to Broadway, in search of the happiness she once knew.
The tumultuous changes that follow lead her to the triumph of new
success . . . and the promise of her greatest love.

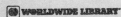